THIS IS THE LIFE

THIS IS THE LIFE

ALEX SHEARER

blue door

Blue Door
An imprint of HarperCollins*Publishers*
77–85 Fulham Palace Road,
Hammersmith, London W6 8JB

First published in Great Britain by Blue Door 2014

A catalogue record for this book is
available from the British Library

ISBN: 978-0-00-752971-1

Set in Minion by Palimpsest Book Production Ltd,
Falkirk, Stirlingshire

Printed and bound in Great Britain by
Clays Ltd, St Ives plc

MIX
Paper from
responsible sources
FSC™ C007454

For Bob, who understood the problem.

1

HAIRCUT

We walked in and the two Chinese girls who ran the place looked up and gave us a nod. They were both busy and neither of them seemed too pleased to see us. But Louis was oblivious to that, so we sat down anyway and waited our turn.

Soon as we sat down, the two Chinese girls started working very slowly, as if there were a competition between them to be the last to finish. The prize for coming in first would be to have Louis as the next customer, and neither of them wanted that. So they both attended diligently to detail and went snip-snip-snipping with fine precision and they used plenty of combing and lots of changes of blade sizes and plenty of holding up of the mirror for a look at the back of the head.

By this time Louis was all beard, moustache, straggly

hair and eyebrows. The eyebrows arched quizzically, or, if Louis had been fiddling with them, which he did, they pointed up like small devil's horns. I didn't think he had had a shave or haircut in six months, maybe longer. Nor had he trimmed his beard in any way. He looked like a wild man, like one of those rough sleepers you feel part sorry for, part afraid of, and part repelled by.

The remains of some ancient dinners were hiding in the moustache. No wonder the Chinese girls were working slowly. If I'd been a Chinese girl, I'd have worked slowly too, or have closed the place early, or simply have said no and have pointed at the door.

But they were too polite, or kind, or resigned, or simply didn't want to lose the business. Finally, one of the seated customers was done with. The taller Chinese girl – who also appeared to be the older – shook hair from the gown and then invited us to step forwards.

'She's ready for you, Louis.'

Louis looked at me in that milky-eyed way he had adopted, and in which fashion he looked at almost everyone. It was a strange look, one of appeal and also of stoical resignation. It took me back half a lifetime, to when we were kids. No, more than half. It was a lifetime. His, at least, and maybe mine too soon – who knows?

'Louis?'

He stood up and took the beanie hat off, handing it to me along with the blue cooler bag he carried his needed possessions in – things like drugs and paperwork and his mobile phone, which he seemed to have forgotten how to use, and his bank card, the number for which he could not remember.

He sat in the barber's chair.

'So what will it be?' the Chinese girl said. She half looked at Louis, but really she was addressing the question to me, and we all knew it. But Louis was an adult and he still had a brain – well, most of one.

'What would you like, Louis? How short? General trim? How about the beard? Short but not too short, maybe? That all right?'

He gave me the milky-eyed look and nodded.

'Short but not too short, please.'

The Chinese girl nodded, and she got to work. If she felt any revulsion or repugnance, she didn't show it. She knew there was something wrong and that Louis wasn't firing on all cylinders, but that maybe he had done once. It wasn't as if he'd always been this way, which would have been a different matter. But it wasn't like that at all.

She seemed to realise all that, and she clipped and snipped almost with respect and reverence for the old Louis, the Louis as he was, Louis as he had been. Not, in all truth, that he had ever been so different. You wouldn't have called him dapper or well-groomed at any stage of his career. (If you could call it a career – maybe random trajectory might have been better.)

But she cut away, first with the scissors and then with the electric trimmer. Gradually, Louis emerged from behind the disguise, and then suddenly there he was again, just like he'd been when we'd been punching the day-lights out of each other all those years ago. Just older and greyer, that was all. I started to wonder if he hadn't always had that sad, milky, lost and appealing look in his eyes, as if to say life was just one bewildering mystery, and why didn't he fit into it, when he could do so many things, and be good at them too. But nobody ever had an answer to that. Nobody, in my experience, has the answer to much along those lines.

'Eyebrow?'

Louis looked at me again and he raised one of the eyebrows to which the Chinese girl was referring as if to ask my opinion.

'If you could,' I said. 'That would be great.'

It wouldn't be great. It would just be shorter eyebrows. But that's the kind of thing you say to people in shops. It's along the lines of *Have a nice day* and *How are you doing?* and *Awesome* and *No worries* and *No dramas*.

Louis settled back and closed his eyes to let the eyebrow work begin.

I wondered if maybe he was developing cataracts, and that possibly accounted for the milky look that was turning to cream. He already had glaucoma. He'd had a lot of ailments. Maybe he hadn't looked after himself. He'd lived with Bella for fifteen years and Kirstin for seven. She'd moved out ten years ago and he'd spent a solid decade neglecting himself.

The Chinese barber took a comb and trimmers and deftly cut back the mad eyebrows. By the time she'd finished, Louis looked normal and sane. He wasn't the wild man any more. You even realised that he was almost good-looking. In fact I wondered if he wasn't better-looking than me and thought that he might be. But then, as any not so good-looking person can tell you, looks aren't every-thing.

It took her a while to do it all, and when she was finished, she did the business with the two mirrors and the back of the head. But when she had done, she didn't charge any extra, just the standard rate. Louis looked at me to pay, so I took the money out of his wallet and the Chinese girl seemed surprised when I gave her a tip, though she plainly deserved one.

We thanked her and left and I handed Louis his wallet back.

'I gave her a tip,' I told him. 'With your money. Hope that was all right.'

He didn't respond, just put the wallet away in his blue cool bag.

'How do the bits and pieces look?' he asked, taking a glance at his reflection in a window. The sun was high and bright and the shop windows were like mirrors.

'Fine,' I said. 'She did a good job.'

'Where's my hat?' Louis said.

I gave it to him and he put it on.

'Aren't you too warm in that?' I asked.

'It's all going to fall out anyway,' he said.

I saw that the brand name on his beanie was Piping Hot.

As he put the hat on, I saw his scar clearly for the first time. It had healed well but still looked ugly. I didn't like the thought of it – of having your skull cut open and a part of your brain taken out, even an infected part.

'Let's go and have a coffee,' Louis said. 'I'll shout you a coffee.'

Louis always had the knack of sounding particularly generous, even when he wasn't actually doing that much.

'I'll stand you a coffee,' he said. 'Or lunch.'

5

We walked on down the street. The Brisbane suburb looked American to me; it had that wide-spaced look, with buildings sprawling out instead of up – like some outback town.

'How about here?'

There were cafés everywhere, but this one had plenty of free tables outside. The waitresses were young and friendly. Not Chinese, maybe Malaysian. But I guess they were all Australian really. They'd just started off as Chinese and Malaysian once, and now they were Australian, same as the one-time British and Irish and Greek and Scottish were. It was a broad church, you might say.

We sat at a table and a waitress brought a menu over.

'Can you light one of those gas burners?' Louis asked. 'I'm cold.'

'You want to sit inside?' I asked him.

'No. But I'd like the burner.'

'Sure,' the waitress said. 'No worries.'

And she opened a valve and pressed some button to light the burner up.

When she'd gone I said to Louis, 'How come no one here has any worries?' He looked at me, puzzled. 'Everyone says "No worries",' I told him. 'I can't believe they don't have any.'

He didn't respond. He kind of looked right through me. But that was nothing new. He'd always done that, since we were kids.

He was staring at the menu but couldn't make sense of it, so I read it out.

'I'll have that,' he said. But then he wanted to know the price, and when I told him, he almost changed his mind.

'I'll pay,' I told him.

'It's all right,' he said. 'But it's expensive.'

'It's the cost of living, Louis,' I said.

And what else did he have to spend it on anyway? And how long left did he have to spend it? The world was full of people with money worries, but there were also people with no money worries at all, yet they were still worried – they were worried that something might happen and their money wouldn't be able to fix it.

I sometimes think that if you started listing all the things that money can't fix, it would be even longer than the list of things it can.

Sometimes money is as much use as rocks in the desert, when what you need is a glass of cold water.

2

TERRI

Terri has two stories – or, rather, she has one story, but there are two versions of it, with contradictory endings, and this is permutation number one.

The first time I heard about Terri was when Louis rang me one morning. It was always morning when he rang – morning my time, late evening his. He'd have got back home from whatever particularly crummy job he was doing that day. Louis had a good brain and he had a degree and a masters and an engineering diploma, but for all that he worked in low-skilled, low-paid employment, for, like the character of Biff Loman in Arthur Miller's play *Death of a Salesman*, it was as though he couldn't 'get a hold on life'.

He told me once that he didn't work in the field he was qualified for as he 'didn't like the politics'. The problem with that, as far as I was concerned, is that there are politics everywhere. You could have the dirtiest, least-respected, lowest-paid job going, but there's still politics in it; there's still a boss, still co-workers. You can't get away from politics any more than you can get away from other people. It can be done, but it's not easy. You'd need to be a hermit.

But, in common with many people who don't fit into the world as it is, Louis just had to do things right. No slacking, idling or cutting corners. The bummest job had to be done just so, and he was always complaining about bad management and employees who didn't care, even when he was working as a maintenance man on the minimum wage, or in a factory somewhere, on the assembly line. Louis always appeared to know what needed to be done to run a business properly, he just couldn't seem to do it for himself. He tried setting up on his own a couple of times, but lost money on both occasions. Yet, for all that he was so well qualified and educated, he believed that working with your hands was superior to working with your mind for some reason. Maybe he thought it was more genuine, more authentic. And the irony of that was that all our parents had ever wanted for both of us was an education and an escape from the drudgery of factory labour and manual toil.

Anyway, he called up and I answered the phone. There had been a time when calls were rare, just Christmas and birthdays and emergency measures. But the cost of international calls had come down and we spoke frequently, maybe once a week or a fortnight.

'Hey!' he said.

'Hi, Louis,' I said, a little annoyed at being interrupted

at what I was doing but trying to conceal it. You can't blame people for ringing at inconvenient times. When you call them it's probably the same. 'How's it going?'

'You won't believe what happened,' he said. And then, as usual, having said that, he fell silent, like he wanted me to extract the information, like he was the winkle and I had a pin.

'What happened, Louis?'

'I went round to see Terri this afternoon,' he said.

I felt I ought to know who Terri was, but I'd forgotten.

'Terri? Who's she again?'

'Terri, you know, who was married to Frank.'

'Ah, Frank. Right.'

I should have known who Frank was too.

'That I used to work with. The roofing.'

'Right, yeah.'

I recollected now. Louis had been in business a while with Frank and they fixed roofs together. It all went wrong when Frank acquired a dog and brought it along with him to the sites. It was a traumatised rescue dog and it barked incessantly. The barking drove Louis mad and he threw a spanner at the dog one day, which got Frank mad, and the working partnership didn't last much longer after that.

Terri had had enough of Frank too, as his drinking had moved from heavy to alcoholic levels. So she divorced him and she bought a small bungalow in a retirement village. She wasn't so young any more, but who was? And she was still attractive and had the proverbial heart of gold.

'So why'd you go round to see Terri? Just visiting?'

'No, she called me about her guttering, asked me if I

could fix it. It had come loose. There's supposed to be some maintenance guy round there for all that, but he's up to his eyeballs. So I took a ladder and went over with the ute after work.'

Louis had a ute – a utility vehicle, a battered old Nissan van with a flat-bed trailer and a silver aluminium box screwed to the flat-bed, in which you could keep tools, and which you could secure with a padlock.

'So was that okay?'

Long pause.

'Yeah. I fixed the gutter and she asked if I'd like to have a cup of tea, so we had some tea and we were sitting there talking, you know, about Frank and what have you—'

'How is Frank?'

'He's in hospital. He's got diabetes now and something wrong with his liver. He kept coming round and wanting me to go drinking. I'd just have a couple of beers, but that wasn't enough for him. He'd bring Scotch as well, and when I refused to drink any more, the last time he came round, he lost his temper and we had a row. And I haven't seen him since.'

'Ah.'

'Anyway, I was sitting there with Terri, and I don't know what got into me or what came over me, but right out of the blue I suddenly said and I don't know why, I said, Terri, would you like to go to bed with me?'

Silence then, like Louis wanted me to ask a question or needed some prompt to continue. I wanted to sound politely curious but not pruriently nosy.

'Wow, well, that's pretty direct, Louis. No kind of preamble then? Just straight out with the main question.'

'Well, I don't know what came over me. It just came out.'

It had to have been about seven years since he'd split up with Kirstin. I wondered if he'd been celibate all that time, but that's not the kind of question you ask your brother.

'So how did she react? What did she say?'

'Well—'

I heard a faint but colourful chuckle.

'Well – she said okay.'

'Really?'

'Yeah.'

'Just like that!'

'Yeah. Just like that!'

'Were you surprised?'

'I was shocked at myself for saying it!'

'Well – well done.'

That was pretty inappropriate, but I didn't know what else to say right then.

'Yeah,' Louis agreed, then went silent again, as if maybe fishing for further queries or compliments.

'So – eh – how did that go?'

'Great. And then she asked me to stay to dinner.'

'Least she could do,' I said.

'I mean, I've known Terri for years,' Louis said. 'And always liked her. But not, you know—'

'In that way?'

'No. But just sitting there, well, I don't know what came over me.'

'Lust?' I suggested. But Louis just laughed.

'I'm going back to see her again next week,' he said.

'So it could be a regular thing.'

'Have to see,' he said.

I still had the feeling that he would have appreciated a few more questions but I couldn't think of any. And he never asked me about my sex life. In fact Louis never asked me much about my own life at all. His baseline appeared to be that my life was okay and further enquiries were not necessary and would have been superfluous.

'Well, I hope it all works out,' I said.

'Yeah,' Louis said, and he was sounding a little pleased with himself now, I thought, as if he was the only man in the world to have persuaded a woman into bed, which annoyed me somewhat, as I'd done a bit of that too in my time, in a modest way, but who hasn't?

We chatted a little while longer and then we hung up, promising to talk again soon.

It was my turn to call and I rang him a couple of weeks later.

'How's it going, Louis? How are things with Terri?'

'Oh, okay. Okay.'

'Still seeing her?'

'Oh yes. I go round once a week and help out at the bungalow and do a little decorating or whatever, and then stay for dinner and, you know – do the business.'

'Do the business?'

'You know, do the business.'

'You've got such a poetic way with you, Louis.'

'Well, you know, whatever you want to call it.'

'So it's all going fine.'

'Seems to be.'

'Good.'

And I was pleased and to quite an extent relieved that

Louis had someone else to unload his woes on, someone with a warm and sympathetic and absorbent shoulder on which to cry. I wondered if they'd move in together, he and Terri. But next time he called, things were under stress.

'Hi, Louis, how's it going?'

'Ah – not too bad.'

'How's Terri?'

'Aw, okay. I don't see so much of her.'

'Why's that? I thought you were getting on.'

'Well, I got a bit pissed off, to be honest.'

To cut a long one short, whenever Louis went round to see Terri she had some little chore waiting for him – a dripping tap to be fixed, a washer to be put on, a sash cord to be replaced. And then, one afternoon, it was a favour for a neighbour, and then another neighbour, for the street seemed to be full of women on their own, ex-wives and widows, who all had small jobs around the house needing done by somebody both handy and reliable.

According to Louis – by implication, if not outright expression – the price of sex was some initial house maintenance, and he was starting to feel resentful; he was starting to feel used.

'She always needs something done,' he complained. 'Or, if not her, one of her friends. And I've already done a day's work. Then I'm going round there and spending another couple of hours unblocking drains or whatever. I'm just getting a bit pissed off.'

Next time we spoke, he hadn't seen Terri since the last time we'd talked. Intimacy was over. But they remained friendly. She even offered to have Louis to come and live with her for his last few months. But he wouldn't go. He wanted to stay independent, and maybe he was worried about the DIY.

So that was his version. But there is another.

3

PLUMBING

We were sitting in Louis' living room, which was all red, dust-matted carpet and Salvation Army furniture with the price stickers still on, and cheap plastic curtains that didn't quite fit the windows, and which were coming off the end of the tracking for lack of stops.

The hand-basin in the bathroom took an hour to drain, so each time you used it, it filled up. You'd brush your teeth and spit out the toothpaste into the sink and the stuff would stay there and you couldn't wash it away. The kitchen sink was the same. In the shower you had exactly one minute before the tray filled up and began to overflow.

I said we should get a plumber around but Louis was against it.

'It's screwed,' he said. 'It's no use. We're screwed. The whole thing's screwed.'

I'd been trying to encourage him with tales I'd read on the internet of long-term survivors, people who'd had the surgery and the radio and the chemo and had lived on for five, six, seven years and were still going. He appeared to make an effort to believe me, and I thought I saw a flash of optimism in the milky eyes, but then he got upset about the drugs he had to take and whether he'd taken some out of sequence.

'We're screwed,' he said. 'It's no good. We're screwed.'

I tried to convince Louis that we weren't screwed.

'They've got us by the balls and curlies,' he said.

'We're not screwed, Louis,' I said. 'They don't have us by the balls and curlies. We're not without resources, are we? We've come this far and look what we've survived. We've got through all that and we're still going.'

'Maybe,' Louis said. 'But now we're screwed.'

'We're not, Louis,' I said. 'We're not screwed at all. We could have years yet. All right, I'm not saying it's not serious, but there's people who've got through it and survived. There can be good times ahead. And we can get a plumber round.'

'No point. It's screwed,' Louis said.

'Louis, there's a blockage in a pipe somewhere, that's all it is. A plumber can fix it. It's a half-hour job. I'll ask Don, your neighbour, if he can recommend a plumber and get him round.'

'No use,' Louis said. 'We're screwed.'

I went round to see Don anyway and got a number for Barry the plumber and I called him up.

'Sure, I'll be round Thursday, mate. No worries.'

No worries, I thought. That'll be the day.

But it didn't cheer Louis up much. He still said we were screwed, and by then I was starting to agree with him, though I never said as much.

He was right, of course. We are screwed. Every single one of us. People go on so much about winning and being winners and coming in first and all the rest of it. But we all have to lose in the end and the best we can hope for is to go gracefully. Everyone dies. Death comes for us all. We're all screwed. We'll all stop functioning properly sooner or later. So Louis was right.

On the other side of the coin, though, when I suggested getting a fan heater to warm the chilly Australian winter evenings – not exactly cold by northern European stand-ards, but cool enough – Louis was against that too. He said, 'We don't need any heaters, we're tough.'

'You're tough, Louis,' I told him. 'I'm getting a heater.'

And he'd asked the Malaysian girl to put the burner on at the café, hadn't he?

I went to a shop the next morning and bought two heaters – a convector and a blower. I brought them back and plugged them in. Louis sat in his Salvation Army arm-chair and toasted himself. They got to be inseparable, Louis and that heater. Towards the end of his life, that was one of his firmer friends. He wouldn't have it in the bedroom though. He drew the line at that level of comfort and self-indulgence.

'I'll be all right when I'm under the blankets,' he said. 'You don't have heaters in the bedroom.'

I guess you didn't when you were tough.

I recognised the blankets. I'd seen them before. They'd belonged to our mother. They had to be thirty years old and they were disintegrating. When I tried to wash them, the fibres came apart and blocked the washing machine. I went out and bought some doonas – Australian for duvets. While stripping the bed I got a look at the mattress and went on to the internet to order a new one. It was falling apart. Underneath the mattress was a thick crop of dust growing out of what was left of the carpet.

'Have you got a vacuum cleaner, Louis?' I asked.

'Of course I have,' he said indignantly. 'Of course I have a vacuum cleaner.'

'Where is it?'

'I don't remember,' he said.

We had a look and found it in a cupboard. It was out of a museum.

'Who was the last to use it?' I asked.

'Kirstin,' he said.

'And when did you and she split up?'

'I don't know. Ten years ago?'

'Have you got an iron, Louis?'

'Of course I have an iron!'

'So where is it?'

'I'm going to bed.'

I found the iron in a drawer. I don't know who had been the last to use it. Or if anyone ever had.

Barry the plumber came round on the Thursday and fixed the plumbing. He said the pipe-work was so old that it was blocked up with internal corrosion. He turned off the water, cut out the bad pipe, and replaced it.

Louis said he could easily have done that himself at half the cost. I wanted to ask him why he hadn't done it then. But I never did ask him things like that, as I knew he'd just get angry.

I paid Barry cash which I got out of the wall with Louis' card. We met up outside the pharmacy where we were going to get Louis' drugs. It was dusk and the sun was dipping and the street and vehicle lights were coming on. I handed Barry a wad of folded dollars.

'It's like doing a drug deal or something, Barry,' I said.

'No worries,' he said.

'Thanks for fixing things.'

'No dramas, mate,' he said. 'See you, Louis.'

'See you, Barry,' Louis said.

And Barry drove off in his own ute. Every self-respecting tradesman had one.

'That's good then, Louis,' I said. 'We can have showers and brush our teeth now and do the washing-up in the sink.'

But he just shook his head and peered out at me from under the perpetual beanie hat that always seemed about to slide down over his eyes and blot him out. The world wouldn't see him then and he wouldn't see it.

'Shall we go in and get your prescription?' I said. 'Have you got it there in the bag?'

He turned and pushed the door open. The Asian woman who was the pharmacist there recognised him and said hello. She had infinite patience with Louis, even when the words wouldn't come to him or he was having trouble sorting out all the drugs he had to take. It seemed to me that the place was full of people who were infinitely kind, and most of them not white.

We got back out to the street with the drugs ordered and on the way – to be delivered tomorrow by three o'clock. In those few brief minutes the sun had set completely and the world was in southern-hemisphere winter darkness now, which came suddenly and early.

I saw a curry house with its sign lit up.

'Shall we go and get a curry for dinner, Louis?' I said. 'Is that place any good?'

'It's okay,' he said.

'Shall we go there?'

He didn't answer me, which was a habit of his since childhood. He'd often simply stare at you and not answer your question. Not as if he hadn't heard it, but as though the question could not be answered, or deserved no answer. I could never tell. Maybe he hadn't heard me after all.

'Louis,' I said. 'Shall we have a curry?'

'We're screwed,' he said. 'Completely screwed.'

He turned his back on me and walked towards the neon goddess. I followed and we went into the restaurant. Once again, when we ordered our food, the waitress taking our order said, 'No worries.'

There you have it, I thought. Some say no worries and some say we're screwed. I guessed there had to be a middle ground somewhere. But I didn't know what you'd call it. Or maybe it was just a swinging pendulum, which veered between the two conditions until it finally ran down and came to a halt and you couldn't wind it up again. And when it stopped moving, that was when they buried you, and you were neither one thing nor the other then, just finished, but free from pain.

4

TERRI TWO

At the funeral Terri got up and said some well-meant and well-intended words. I liked her. She seemed like a nice, genuine person, who had felt real affection for Louis and had liked him for himself. We got talking and she said I should come around for a meal before I went home. I said I would take her up on that, and besides Louis had borrowed some bedding from her that I needed to return. So she gave me her number and she told me to call, which I did after a week or so, and I arranged to go round.

I thought we'd maybe go to a restaurant, but she said there was a communal lounge and dining area on site, where the bungalow dwellers could get together once a week if they so desired and eat dinner at trestle tables – all provided at minimal cost.

It was a barn of a place, full of noisy conversations.

There were married and elderly couples there, along with divorcees, singles, and allegedly amorous widows on the lookout for spare men. I found Terri at a table with her friends. She'd saved a space for me, so I sat down and she introduced me, and we all exchanged small talk about the UK and what have you. After the first course, a woman Terri knew wandered over to say hello. Terri introduced us, and as they chatted, the woman remained standing next to where I sat. Next thing I knew she had her hand on my shoulder, then her fingers were in my hair, then she was playing with the lobe of my ear, which sent tingles along my arm. Then she asked me where I lived and when I said the UK, she gave up on me and walked off.

There was no coffee to be had so Terri invited me back to her bungalow. She had a small dog, but it was friendly and nice, and not much of a barker. We drank instant coffee and talked about Louis. We talked about his boiler, which had conked out a decade ago. It had taken him a full ten years to get round to fixing it, and he had lived without hot water all that time, taking invigorating cold showers, even in winter. His washing machine ran off cold water too.

'And yet he was so good at fixing other people's things,' she said.

'Isn't there something about the shoemaker's kids always being badly shod?'

'I suppose,' she said.

We talked some more about Louis and she said how good he had looked after the famous haircut, but that generally speaking he had allowed himself to turn into a wild man.

'I'd look at those eyebrows,' she said, 'and think, Louis,

if you'd just shave that beard off, you'd be quite a hand-some man. He could scrub up really nice. But well, you know Louis . . .'

Louis was always covered in paint. If not him personally, then his clothes. Some people have good, going-out clothes and working clothes. All of Louis' clothes were working clothes, because if a job needed doing, he'd do it, irrespec-tive of what he had on. As a result almost everything he owned had paint or oil daubed on it, and he lived in shorts, even in winter, and his elbows poked out of his unravelled sweaters. He was a take-me-as-I-am kind of man. He was a love-me-or-leave-me guy.

Terri went on to say that he had asked her out to dinner once at Fried Fish, which was an upmarket kind of fish and chip place down near the harbour.

'I thought he'd have got dressed up,' she lamented. 'And I went to a lot of trouble. But he turned up in his ute in his working clothes. I felt I was going out for a meal with the workman,' she said. 'I was so embarrassed.' Then she sighed and said, 'Though I did like your brother. And underneath that beard he could have been quite a handsome man.'

I sneaked a look at my watch and thought that maybe I ought to go. I didn't want to outstay my welcome. They seemed to keep early hours in the bungalow city.

But then, as I was about to make excuses, Terri said, 'You know, I maybe shouldn't tell you this, but Louis came to see me once, oh, a year or two ago, and he was sitting right where you are now, in that very chair . . .'

We both looked at that very chair I was sitting in, as if it might speak, or somehow bear witness, or disclose its mysteries. But it stayed schtum.

'Yes, he was sitting in that very chair – and I don't know if I should tell you this, but quite out of the blue, I mean, I was so surprised – you know what Louis said to me?'

I did, but felt that I couldn't admit to it.

'He said, Terri, would you like to go to bed with me?'

'Wow,' I said, feeling I had to say something. 'Well, that was Louis for you, always subtle.'

'I was so surprised. So surprised.'

'I bet.'

'Because I'd never ever thought of Louis in that way. I'd always just thought of him as a friend of Frank's. Not to say though that if he'd trimmed that beard and moustache off he wouldn't have been quite a good-looking man.'

'Well, Louis always had a beard,' I said. 'Since his twenties. He'd had that beard a long time.'

'So anyway, I was that taken aback.'

'Absolutely.'

'I didn't know where to look.'

'A very difficult situation,' I agreed. 'To have come out with it like that. I mean, no preamble or anything.'

'Not a word. No preliminaries. No what you'd call—'

'Courtship rituals?' I suggested.

'No warning at all.'

'Well, Louis always preferred the direct approach.'

But I was just stalling. I was just trying to keep things on a neutral footing so as not to put her off from telling me what had happened next.

'Well, I did not know what to say,' Terri said.

'Quite an embarrassing situation,' I nodded, 'to be put on the spot like that.'

'And he was looking at me with such sad eyes. He had such sad eyes sometimes, your brother.'

'He had to put drops in them for his glaucoma,' I said. 'In fact I sometimes wondered if it wasn't the roofing that caused it. You know Louis, he'd never wear sunglasses, and up there on those roofs in the Australian sunshine, and it reflecting off the surface. Surely that could damage your eyes.'

'No,' she said. 'They were more like a labrador's eyes. They'd look at you sort of sadly, but affectionately too. And Frank never got glaucoma, but then he drank a lot.'

'I'm not so much of a dog person,' I said. 'Though I had a cat once when my girlfriend left. She went off with my best friend but she left the cat behind. Interestingly, Louis introduced that friend to us and then he went off to Australia. He ruined half the furniture – scratched it to pieces. Cats and sofas are a lethal combination. I think the cat resented me and he'd rather have gone with my ex, only she didn't want him.'

'But what a thing to come out with, I thought,' Terri said. 'Terri, would you like to go to bed with me? Just like that.'

I felt there was nothing I could say now that would have been appropriate. So I just waited.

'Well, once I was over the surprise, I said, Louis – Louis, for us to do a thing like that would spoil a beautiful friend-ship.'

'So you—'

'I just couldn't. I mean, if he'd dressed a little smarter maybe, or had had a shave more often. But you can't expect to live without hot water for ten years and still—'

'No, of course.'

'Maintain normal standards,' Terri said.

'So how did Louis take that?' I asked. 'He was okay, I guess. Because you obviously remained friends.'

'Oh yes,' Terri said. 'I really liked Louis. And so did Frank – until he got the drinking problem.'

I looked at my watch.

'I'd better go,' I said. 'It's late and I'm not so sure of the route in the dark.'

Terri gave me detailed directions for a short cut, but they were so complicated I couldn't follow them, and I went back the way I had come. I was driving Louis' ute, which was a noisy rattle trap with a falling-down window and a heater/cooler fan permanently stuck on high. It also had a quarter of a million miles on the clock. And that was Louis too, always buying old and high maintenance. Even when he could afford better.

I said goodbye to Terri and thanked her for everything and we said we'd keep in touch, though I doubted that we would and I believe she doubted that too.

The last I saw of her was in the rear-view mirror, her and her little dog watching me drive away.

I hadn't said a word to her about Louis' version of events; I'd felt it would have been impolite to mention this contradictory story. But I did wonder which version was true. And I also wondered why she had even mentioned the incident. Did she know that I knew something and she wanted to put me right? Or had she really slept with Louis, but was embarrassed about it, because of his paint-splattered clothes and his torn shorts and his creased T-shirt and his untrimmed beard and his not having been under a hot shower in ten years?

And if her version was the true version, then why had Louis told me a different one? Had it been a tale of wish fulfilment? But he hadn't needed to tell me a single thing about it. If she'd turned him down, he could have kept quiet about that. Only the two of them need ever have known.

So where does the truth lie, and does it really matter?

But I liked Terri. She seemed like a good person to me. Good and kind and generous – someone who'd had a hard life but had come through without cynicism and with her values intact. And she said some nice things at the funeral service, and she didn't have to.

So what the hell. What you are supposed to do anyway, with all the fathomless stories that you'll never get to the bottom of, and all the contradictions? People's lives seem like entangled balls of string, with a thousand knots in them. You'll never unpick them all. The best you can do is just carry on and forget about it. You could drive yourself nuts if you brooded over it. And what good would that do anyone? Least of all yourself.

5

BABIES

Back in my juvenile delinquent days I had been apprehended for tearing the leaves off a rhododendron bush, but had given a false name and address, so the cops had come looking for me and stopped the school bus on the way home into town. I guess I must have been the only person on board who looked guilty, so they said it was me, which it was, but I denied it, and they escorted me off the bus to the police station across the road.

I used to try to sit on the long back seat of the bus with the trouble-makers and no-hopers and those who had aspirations to play the electric guitar but who would probably end up working behind a counter.

Seeing me being taken away, Louis – who was a respectable pillar of society back then, with a prefect's badge and high status as deputy head boy – got off the bus too and accompanied me to the station.

When news got to the school the next day, they said they would expel me for what I had done to the bush, as it was plain I was a bad lot and a corrupting influence and heading for the pan.

Louis went to the headmaster's door and knocked on it and requested an interview, during the course of which he relayed the fact that if I got kicked out, he would leave too, and they didn't want to lose him, so we both stayed.

I should have been grateful, I suppose, but I wasn't particularly, as I hated the place and left anyway after a couple of months. But I appreciated his loyalty, as we hadn't been getting on back then and fought constantly. Once he tried to break a beer glass over my head and told me I treated home like a hotel. I told him it was a pretty poor hotel and not what I was used to – which was a lie, as I'd known nothing else. After that I tried to hit him over his head with a cricket bat, but he was too quick for me. But apart from small skirmishes like that, we got on fairly well.

At one time though, Louis had a religious period and our mother started panicking when he let it be known that he felt he maybe had a vocation and would one day become a priest. Our mother went straight to church and prayed that such a thing should never happen, and God, being bountiful, let that particular cup of woe pass to someone else.

All the same, Louis took possession of the high moral ground and defended it staunchly for several months. When he came across the James Bond paperback I was reading he tore it up and binned it and said reading it was a sin.

I had to tell him that it wasn't even my book, I'd been loaned it, and it was none of his damned business what I read as I would read whatever I liked and he could go and screw himself and he'd better get me another copy soon as I was due to return the book to the boy I'd borrowed it from.

Give him his due, he bought a replacement, but he said I wasn't to look inside it, I was to hand it back and no peeking.

When he was out of the way I read the rest and finished the novel. I couldn't see what all the fuss was about, unless it was the heavy smoking.

But that was Louis for you back in those days, always ready with the judgements and the moral tone, but then he mellowed a little in later life and said the school was a nest of hypocrites after it came to light that half of the Reverend Fathers were now standing accused in their retirement of fiddling with little boys.

All the same we had a big row once that set the tone for the remainder of our relationship when Louis told me that as soon as he got the chance he was going to move abroad and head for another country so as to get away from me. And that was just what he did – though whether I was the prime mover in this or just another incidental annoyance he wanted to get away from I'm unsure. I suspect the latter and bear no hard feelings because if he was pleased to go, I was also relieved he was gone, as it meant I could read my books in peace without the censor looking over my shoulder.

The first place Louis went to was Canada. He got his chemistry degree and then went to Alberta to study for an MSc and teach undergraduates. He met a girl there called Chancelle who had a brain the size of his or maybe even bigger and they both studied chemistry and had a lot of sex, according to Louis, and no doubt some intellectual conversations afterwards. They soon moved in together.

Chancelle was French Canadian and her family supported a free and separate Quebec. They wouldn't speak English to you and made out that they didn't know any, though they did and spoke it like natives when people weren't looking. Louis had to learn some French or they'd have left him out of all the conversations. He got quite fluent as far as I know, though he spoke it with a Canadian accent.

But things went to pot after a few years. Louis got his degree and went to work for a mining company out in the sticks. Chancelle got more deeply involved in French Canadian politics and she and Louis only saw each other at weekends. She began an affair with another French Canadian who was also active on the political front (and, no doubt, the sexual one) and spoke better French than Louis did.

Louis got disillusioned and disgusted and came back home. Like most academically-inclined people who don't know what to do with themselves, he decided to return to university. So he studied for an engineering diploma this time, and when he got it, he moved up north and worked in a straight and proper job for a while, but he got disillusioned and disgusted, as they didn't know how to run a business and there was too much politics and the senior management were wankers.

So he took his savings and bought a narrow boat and sailed it down the canal and moored it in the harbour half a mile from the flat I lived in with a woman I had fallen in love with, on account – amongst other things – of her Scottish accent. The trouble was she was an artist, and her friends were artists, and Louis lived on a boat now, and he got into craft and furniture making and rented a small workshop by the docks. So everyone was a bohemian apart from me, and I had to get up on Monday mornings and go to work, as I was the one paying the rent.

This narrow boat was the first of Louis' wrecks. It needed so much work done to it, it would have been easier to start from scratch and build a new one. It had once been a fire boat on the Birmingham canal. Its engine was situated in the middle of the boat, instead of one of the ends, which is more usual, and it had two drive shafts, so that the boat could go in either direction without the need to turn it around – which can be difficult in a narrow canal when you're in a hurry to put out a fire.

There was no comfort in that boat at all, just a couple of hard bunks and a stove to cook beans on.

'It's a doer-upper,' Louis told me. 'What do you think?'

'I think,' I told him, 'that the trouble with you and your doer-uppers, Louis, is that you never do do them up. You never get round to it, do you? You lose interest and start on something else and you don't finish that either. Because you lose interest again and—'

'I'm thinking of doing it out in mahogany,' Louis said. 'I'll put some partition walls up and get it divided into rooms. Bathroom here, galley there, living quarters here, guest bedroom there.'

'Where are you putting the games room, spa and indoor swimming area, Louis?' I asked. But he ignored me as if I hadn't spoken.

'It's going to be something special once it's done.'

'It'll be something special if it ever does get done. This is the story of your life to date, Louis,' I said. 'Things taken on and not seen through. Great projects started and never completed. Remember that astronomical telescope you were going to make when we were kids?'

'I made a start on it but was trammelled by lack of proper equipment,' he said.

'Louis,' I reminded him, 'you were going to grind your own lenses. And the bits of glass were a yard across and six inches thick.'

'If I was doing it today, I'd do it differently,' Louis said.

'Okay, Louis. If you really want my opinion – and I know you don't – the first thing I'd do to this boat if I were you – apart from sell it – is to put a proper heating system in. Get a wood-burning stove or something. That little cooker is not going to warm this boat. Not once winter comes. It's going to be so cold in here come January that brass will crack.'

'We don't need any stoves,' Louis told me. 'We're tough.'

'You may be tough,' I said. 'But when winter comes I'm going to buy myself a portable gas heater for the flat.'

I seem to recollect that Louis spent a lot of time that winter round at our apartment, sleeping on the sofa. He and my girlfriend Iona got on okay. But then they were both bohemians and weren't paying any rent.

The fact was that when it came to being tough, I only really helped the tough guys out when they were busy. My parents had wanted a girl as their second child, only they hadn't got one, they had got me. According to my mother I was born so scrawny I wasn't expected to live, but live I did. Even now there are people who bear grudges about that. But I can't do anything about it.

Spring came and the air got warmer and Louis went back to his boat. Sometimes the harbour master would move the boat on a whim and Louis would go home after a night in the pub to find his boat gone from its moorings, and he would have to tramp round the harbour looking for it, which could take him an hour or more. He fell in the water a few times, but it was only to be expected and was probably character-building, and it never seemed to do him any harm, apart from the difficulty he had in drying his clothes.

Looking back now, I see that was the start of his sartorial problems and when he first began aiming for the rough-sleeper look, which he seemed to so effortlessly accomplish. He ripped his trousers once and walked round for a week with the leg flapping until Iona sewed it up for him, even though she was a strong feminist and it was old-style women's work.

'You should be able to sew up your own trousers, Louis,' she told him.

'I'm working on it,' he said.

'I thought you were working on your boat,' I told him.

'I'm working on them both.'

He was actually working on neither. He had a new interest, making occasional tables.

'Does that mean the tables are for particular occasions, Louis? Or does it mean you just make them occasionally?'

He just looked at me as if I wasn't there and didn't answer.

I still have one of his occasional tables, sitting right there in the dining room. Tile inlaid surface and pine legs. It's warped and buckled a little with the passing of the years, but it's lasted the course. It's outlived its maker in any event. It wasn't that Louis couldn't do things, it was that he couldn't make money out of them. Nor was he a natural craftsman, he was more one by ambition and willpower. He lost his temper with inanimate objects quite a lot. I could be wrong but I believe that natural craftsmen don't do that – they know how to bend the inanimate to their will, and how to persuade it into shape with cajoling and subtlety and cunning. And that's the craft of it.

Louis' savings slowly dwindled and he couldn't be a bohemian any more. He went and got a manual job assembling generators. It was just a stop-gap thing, like so many of those jobs were. He stop-gapped for almost the rest of his life. And maybe I'm wrong about his stopping being a bohemian. Maybe he was just a bohemian in a nine to five job; the bohemianism was in his soul.

He never did do the boat up, nor did he ever install a stove. He ended up hauling the boat out of the water and chopping it up for firewood.

But before that, we had a crisis.

The phone rang in the flat and it was a woman with a French-sounding accent.

'Hello,' she said. 'I was given this number and I want to speak to Louis.'

'Who's calling?' I said.

'Chancelle,' she said. 'I'm at the airport and have flown over to get back together with Louis and I want to have his babies.'

'Who gave you my number?'

'Your mother.'

'I see. Well, Louis doesn't live here, Chancelle—' She stifled a sob. 'That is, he lives near, but this is my place.'

'But I have come all this way—'

'Wouldn't it have been better to take soundings first?'

'What is this – take soundings?'

'Chancelle, have you communicated with Louis about this? You haven't seen each other in, what, three, four years? Have you written to him? Was he expecting you?'

'I love Louis so much and want to have his babies.'

'Well, you'll need to speak to Louis about that. I don't know where he stands on babies. That's something you'll need to discuss.'

'I am coming to see him.'

'Chancelle—'

'I am getting on the bus.'

'Chancelle, you don't even know—'

'Your mother gave me your address. I'll be there tonight. Tell Louis I love him.'

The phone went dead.

'Who was that?' Iona said.

'Chancelle,' I explained. 'Louis' ex from Canada. She's landed at Heathrow.'

'What does she want?'

'She wants to have his babies.'

Iona gave me a strange and narrow-eyed look. I didn't know then that she wanted to have my babies. But I didn't want any babies at that time in my life. Eventually despairing of never having any babies, Iona went off to have them with somebody else.

'Well, is he expecting her?'

'I don't think he's heard from her in years.'

I found Louis down at the docks, chewing the fat with his neighbours. Wherever you go in the world you will find men with boats chewing the fat. They rarely venture anywhere. Their boats are usually out of the water and need something doing to them. There's some rubbing down going on, or some filling in, or they're painting the hull in de-fouling liquid. The maintenance is long and the voyages are few. But that's not the point. The point is the old boats and the tea and the bacon sandwiches and a place to go come the Bank Holidays and the empty vacation times and the long, hot, eternal summer days, when you can take your shirt off and let your belly hang out and show the passers-by your tattoos.

'Louis,' I said. 'I just got a phone call. It's Chancelle and she's landed at Heathrow and she's coming down here to have your babies.'

Louis looked panic-stricken.

'She's coming here?'

'Right now. Even as we speak she's on the bus and throwing her birth-control devices out of the window.'

'Jesus,' Louis said.

'What do you want me to say?'

'I'm going to have to go,' Louis said. And he went on board his boat and started packing a bag. He had bought an old rusty car by now. He got it cheap as it had three hundred thousand miles on the clock.

'Louis,' I said, following him. 'You can't just disappear and leave me to deal with her. What am I going to say? She wants to have your babies.'

'Well, I don't want to have her babies.'

'You what?'

He threw a grey towel into a bag.

'That is I don't want her to have mine. I haven't heard from her in years. She's crazy.'

'I guess the separatist politics must have gone wrong.'

'I'm not seeing her.'

'Louis, where are you going?'

'Walking,' he said. 'In Wales.'

'Louis,' I said. 'You can't just run off and disappear and leave me to deal with a woman who's travelled six thousand miles or however far it is to have your babies.'

'Watch me.'

'Louis, it isn't fair.'

He paused in packing his bag.

'Remember the school bus? When you got arrested?'

'Maybe, Louis. But who's the delinquent now?'

'Blood's thicker,' he said.

'Louis—'

'It's your turn to do me a favour,' he said.

'Louis, I've done you favours. You've spent the whole winter in front of my portable gas fire and my girlfriend sewed your trousers up.'

He zipped the holdall and squared up to me. He was no taller than I was, but he was a stone or two heavier, and it wasn't fat, it was muscle. Though when it came to a fight we were fairly equal, for though he was the stronger, I was the more desperate man. I think I had discovered that when we were children. And the reason I was more desperate and fought more ferociously was because I knew I was the weaker.

'It's little to ask from your only brother. It's little to ask. I'd do it for you.'

'You wouldn't, Louis. You'd tell me to face up to my responsibilities.'

'I'm going walking in the Black Mountains,' he said. 'I'll be back Thursday or when she's gone, whichever is the sooner. I'll call.' He hustled me out of the boat and locked it. Then he had a thought.

'You want to come with me?' he said. 'You like walking, don't you?'

'Louis, I have to go to work. And how come you can take time off?'

'They owe me holidays.'

'Louis, what am I going to say to Chancelle about your babies?'

'Tell her I had a vasectomy.'

And off he went. He had a little trouble getting the car started and almost suffocated the both of us with all the black smoke. But that was Louis for you – Louis and his vehicles. If they didn't burn oil and belch out fumes and break down regularly, he wouldn't buy them.

Chancelle turned up that evening and was nigh inconsolable. She had put on a lot of weight and looked as though she were expecting babies already, quite a few of them, or at the very least twins.

She sat and sobbed and sobbed, but I had to be hard and I told her it was over and there was nothing anyone could do, as Louis had gone off to the Black Mountains and he didn't want to have babies with her at any price.

Iona held her hand and I made some tea and then we sent out for a pizza. She stayed the night on the sofa, and when I explained that Louis had spent the winter there, she seemed comforted slightly.

The next morning she got a bus to London and that was the last we saw or heard of her.

Louis rang the following evening and asked if it was safe to come home.

'Louis,' I said, 'when you say "home", where do you mean exactly?'

'Where the heart is,' he said.

He could throw me like that sometimes by coming out with the completely unexpected.

'I've met someone,' he said. 'With blonde hair.'

'What? In the Black Mountains?'

'She's a backpacker from New Zealand. I've invited her to stay on my boat for a while.'

'I hope she doesn't feel the cold then, Louis.'

'No way,' he said. 'We're tough.'

6

OLD BLACK DOG

I t's easy to think that you know where and when the rot started. With the so-called benefit of hindsight. Always presuming it is a benefit and not the opposite, some kind of handicap or millstone thing around your neck.

I was eleven years old and Louis was twelve and our father was dying upstairs in a room we were no longer allowed to enter on the grounds that he wanted us to remember him as he was. The flaw in this prohibition was that he hadn't looked so great the last time we had seen him, and if I had to remember him in that condition, then I could equally have remembered him in his last few days and been no more the traumatised.

He'd been suffering from lung cancer due to twenty to thirty a day hand-rolled for years and years.

Whenever I see these tobacco company executives in

their nice suits and white shirts and sober ties, as they make their justifications and announce their profits and explain how they are opening up fresh markets in the new world, I think the sons-of-bitches should be boiled in oil for all the suffering they have caused. And I wonder if they smoke, or if they would want their own children to smoke, and I firmly believe it's the last thing they would want, to find their own offspring hanging out of the bathroom window with cigarettes in their mouths.

Anyway, he spent his last few weeks getting increasingly yellow and burning holes in the sheets to our mother's fear and dismay, for he carried on smoking right to the bitter end – and it was bitter. She was afraid he'd set fire to the bed and the whole place would go up, and then we'd all die of smoke inhalation together.

So it wasn't a question of if, just when. And I came home from school one afternoon to find Louis waiting at the back of the house. For the front door was a thing we never used except for visitors, or when the police came round to talk about the rhododendron bush.

Louis had been waiting for me to return, for though we were at the same school, we were in different classes, and he always took the high road home, whereas I took the low road, with its many distractions, and so I rarely got back before him.

'He's dead,' Louis told me.

I shrugged, for we were tough.

'That so?' I said.

And we stood there a while, and then we went inside, and our mother was in the kitchen, and the rest is pretty much of a blank.

After the funeral we came home, the three of us, to our sad, shabby, rented home. I wouldn't say it reeked of poverty, but there was certainly an odour of the stuff around the place and opening the windows and letting the air in didn't ever make a huge amount of difference.

Our mother began taking her best and only jacket off and starting in on the tea-making, which was her recourse in all contingencies.

'Well, Louis,' she said. 'I guess that you're the man of the house now.'

I don't blame her for what she said in her grief and loneliness, but to this day I'm convinced it was the beginning of at least half of the trouble. It's a hard job to have to take on, being the man of the place at twelve years old. But Louis had to shoulder the burden. The corollary of that, of course, was all the resentment it created in me. I bit my lip and kept my mouth shut, but inside my heart was boiling, and I thought no way is my brother going to be my father, and I was stubborn ever after, and went to the bad for a while, and took up attacking rhododendron bushes.

What brought it all back to mind was when I first got to Louis' place in Australia and walked in through the door and saw him in his beanie hat with a quarter of his mind gone and the next thing I saw was his kettle – which deserves a digression of its own at another time – and I clapped my eyes on his fridge.

There were things living in that fridge that even medical science didn't know about. Its age was incalculable. They didn't make fridges like that any more. Maybe they never had and Louis had constructed it himself out of old spare parts and tree bark.

But it wasn't just the mould, the grime, the gone-off food, the brown grapefruit, the rust, the smell and all the rest. It was the fridge magnets. There were half a dozen of them, all of them rusty too, and they bore messages saying: Depression – you are not alone. And they had phone numbers on them of people you could call and could talk to. But whether Louis had ever called and spoken to anyone, I never asked. I just thought that well, the old black dog was back, or maybe it had never gone away. I knew that Louis had always had it snapping at his heels. But maybe it had got him by the throat lately, or even now was hiding in the house somewhere, under the bed in the deep, deep dust, or growling down in the basement. Or maybe that was it making noises up in the loft. Only when I later asked Louis about the loft noises that were keeping me awake, he said it was possums.

So I asked why he didn't get rid of them, but he said they didn't bother him too much, so maybe he liked their company. I asked him what they were doing up there that made so much noise.

'They're having a root,' he said. 'They're rooting away, making more possums.'

'Louis,' I said. 'What use are even more possums to you? You can't even cope with the ones you already have.'

But he just shrugged and wouldn't do anything about them. And I didn't want to buy poison or anything, for I drew the line at poisoning possums, though had it been rats, I wouldn't have thought twice. So we just had to put up with the racket, but it left you feeling tired in the mornings, and maybe it made the possums feel tired too.

'Why can't they have a root before they go to sleep, Louis?'

'That's how they are,' he said.

'But you know what it's like when you wake up in the morning when there's two of you.'

'Farts and bad breath and stale alcohol,' Louis said, for he was always one to cut to the chase and never mind the niceties. 'But you do it anyway. Though in a possum's case, there maybe isn't the stale alcohol.'

'Louis,' I said. 'Are you all right?'

And I meant regarding the fridge stickers. But some things, even when we reached out for them, we never really grabbed hold of. You know that famous painting, in the Sistine Chapel, called 'The Creation', with God and Man reaching out for each other but their hands don't quite connect. That was how we communicated.

'Let's have a drink,' Louis said.

'What do you want?'

'Cuppa tea,' he said.

'All right. Sit down and I'll make us one.'

That was when I noticed the kettle.

'Louis,' I said. 'What's the deal with the kettle?'

'What do you mean?' he said. 'What's wrong with it?'

Louis lived inside but really he was camping out.

On his grease- and left-overs-encrusted gas stove stood a blackened kettle. It was one of the old-fashioned kind that you boil over a hob. Louis did have electricity, but it didn't extend as far as his hot drink requirements.

'Louis,' I said. 'This kettle has no handle.'

'Broken off,' he said.

'Louis, when did the handle break off?'

He gave another of his shrugs. He had square, solid, powerful shoulders. If you'd been thinking of a fight with him, you'd think twice.

'I don't know. Few years ago.'

He went and sat in his Salvation Army armchair and opened up his blue cooler bag and fished out some eye drops for his glaucoma.

'Louis, how do you pour the water out when the kettle has boiled?'

'Tea towel,' he said, with annoyance in his voice, as if I was being deliberately obtuse.

'So let me get this right, Louis. You have lived for unspecified years with a kettle with no handle that you have to wrap a tea towel around to pour the water out of?'

'I'm doing my eyes!'

'Louis, how much is a kettle?'

'I've been busy.'

'I'm going to buy one tomorrow.'

'Don't waste your money.'

'Louis, a kettle with a handle will make life easier, right? If you make your own life easier, you're not wasting your money. You're just spending it on improving your situation, right?'

'We don't need handles on our kettles, we're—'

'Louis, not having a handle on your kettle doesn't make you tough. Being tough has nothing to do with kettle handles. Scott of the Antarctic went to the South Pole, Louis. Was he tough?'

'You'd need to ask him.'

'Louis, I've seen pictures of Scott of the Antarctic and his men in their hut at the South Pole and I swear to God, Louis, that they had a handle on their kettle. They might even have carried a spare handle, for all I know.'

'Are you making the tea or aren't you?'

So I made the tea. I had to scour the mugs first. They were stained a deep tannin brown inside.

'There you go.'

'Thanks.'

'I'm buying a new kettle tomorrow, Louis. While you're at the hospital, I'm buying a new kettle.'

'Don't waste your money.'

But I didn't listen to him and I did what I wanted. Who did he think he was anyway? My father or someone?

We ended up with two new kettles. One electric, and one for the gas stove – with a handle. I edged the old one out of the house gradually. First I left it out on the veranda. Then, when Louis didn't notice that, I carried it down the stairs and left it in the garden. After a week I moved it next to the bin. The following week I put it in the bin. Then, on the Tuesday, I put the bin out for collection.

On Wednesday, when Louis was back from his radio-therapy, he began mooching around the kitchen.

'You lost something, Louis?' I asked.

'My kettle,' he said. 'Where's my kettle?'

'Right there,' I said, pointing at the electric one plugged into the wall. 'Or did you mean this one?' And there was the new and shiny blue one on the gas hob.

'No. My kettle. My kettle.'

'You mean the old burnt black and crusty one with no handle?'

'My kettle.'

'Louis, I didn't think you wanted it any more. I didn't think we needed it. As we have these nice new kettles. So I'm afraid – it's gone.'

'You threw it out? You threw out my kettle?'

'Louis, it was dangerous, you could have scalded yourself, or set fire to the place, you had to wrap a tea towel around it. It was a liability.'

He just looked at me through his milky eyes, now filled with infinite reproach, and I felt like some kind of murderer for what I had done.

'Louis, I didn't know it meant that much to you. I thought it was just an old kettle.'

Without another word, he turned his back on me, and he went to his room and lay down on his bed. The mix of chemo and radiotherapy was very tiring and he spent a lot of the day asleep.

I felt bad. I realised what I had done. It was part of Louis I had thrown away. For years Louis had been the man with the kettle with no handle. People had come round and he had made them a coffee or a tea or a herbal something. And he had poured out their drinks, first carefully wrapping the dirty, scorched old tea towel around the body of the kettle. And they'd watched him do so, and everyone knew that Louis was the man with the kettle without a handle. And so it had been for many years. There had been talk and conversation and many a long hour of putting the world to rights, there in that choked and cluttered kitchen that had seen neither floor cloth nor mop for a decade.

But that had been Louis. That had been part of who he was.

'You know, Louis, don't you? The guy with the beard and the kettle.'

Now he only had the beard left and that had been to the barber's.

I felt bad, like a tyrant, like one who had taken advantage of vulnerabilities. But I couldn't bring the kettle back. It had gone to the dump and even if I searched I would never find it. It was there with all the other long-gone and inadequate domestic appliances. True, I had bought him a new one, but what use was new when it wasn't what you loved?

I don't have much advice to give anyone; I've learned very little in my life; but here's my gem of wisdom. Don't take a dying man's kettle away. You won't be doing him any favours. Nor yourself either.

7

FRIED FISH

Louis had a friend called Halley who was one of the bohemian types and who lived up in the hills forty minutes from the city, with trees for company and scrub turkeys and wallabies, and what sounded like perpetual wind chimes but which turned out to be bell birds – a kind of myna bird with a piercing call which would drive the overly sensitive to insanity in under a week.

Halley made a living from picture frames and he lived in a shed that he had built himself on some land he had bought. This wasn't like a European shed, it was an Australian shed, a far larger and more substantial thing. Louis had put the roof on it. Close to the shed stood a barn, which Louis had also put the roof on, and which contained timber of all sorts – at least all sorts suitable for the making of picture frames.

The frames were fine and artistic things, skilfully crafted. But it was a hand-to-mouth game. Halley said his profits were small and his hours were long. He too drove a ute, but it only had a fifth of a million miles on the clock, so it was almost in showroom condition.

The track he lived up was so steep and lacking in bite on a wet day that you would need someone to sit in the back of your truck to put weight over the rear axle, otherwise you'd be skidding back down again in a hurry or ending up in the ditch.

Like Louis, Halley was also a man of some education, interesting CV, and of varied and floundered relationships. He was also one to whom the odour of the nine to five smelt unpleasant, and he would work eight to six or even longer to avoid getting tangled up in it.

They'd met up at a craft market where Halley sold his frames and where, for a time, Louis had gone into the handmade jewellery business. He spent the week threading beads and the weekend selling them. But it made so little money that the nine to five and the factory walls closed around him again. Louis had degrees and a fine mind and could solve problems others couldn't even understand, but he always had trouble making a living.

There used to be a bumper sticker once that read: If you're so clever, why aren't you rich?

I wondered about this and what the answer to the question was. I eventually got it. Being rich is not necessarily the product of intelligence. In fact, if being rich is what you want, then being clever won't of itself be enough. It might even be too much – a handicap of a kind. If you want to make money you can't afford to take too much into consideration, only what is relevant. If you think too much or too deeply, you can be frozen, maybe from a plethora of choice, maybe from anxiety.

There are people with just enough brains to keep them out of institutions walking around with billions, while men with quantum physics on their minds are buying their clothes from charity shops.

Once a week Halley came into town and rode his bike along the river, then he headed for Louis' place, where they would sit in the kitchen with a six-pack of Little Creatures Pale Ale, and put global matters into perspective.

Halley had a married sister called Barbara, who lead a straighter life, and who was married to Derek, a heavy-set extrovert with a booming voice and many opinions and who had once had a fine occupation as a fixer for a multi-millionaire and who had always flown club-class. But he and the millionaire had fallen out and Derek had seen and felt the parting of the ways and now had a new job working the phones as a debt chaser. He still maybe hankered after the club-class days and found them hard to leave behind.

Barbara and Derek lived on the south side of the city in a smart house with cool tiled floors, not far from the harbour. They had dogs but no children, although they did have Halley and Barbara's ageing mother to live with them. Halley was a regular visitor, and Louis had become a family friend.

They would all spend Christmas together, eating turkey out in the hot Australian sunshine, while Derek did the basting or prised the top off another bottle, his voice booming as he barbecued the ham.

*

Halley turned up one day with a supply of foods which he had discovered from the internet were good for tumours. There were a lot of oranges and ginger and cranberries. Louis never touched any of it and left the fruit to rot. I threw the stuff out with the kettle and didn't tell Halley anything.

'Derek's suggesting meeting up for lunch at the weekend down at Fried Fish. Bring your brother,' Halley said.

It wasn't really a question of Louis bringing his brother at all. It was a matter of his brother bringing him.

They'd taken Louis' licence away the day they found the lump. He'd called me a few times over the preceding weeks, complaining of headaches and that his memory was going and that he was having trouble reading now and couldn't understand what was going on.

'Louis, it sounds to me like you've had some kind of a mini-stroke. You need to go to the doctor.'

He went, eventually, and the doctor sent him for a scan. He took a morning off work to get the scan done. When it was finished the woman operating the machine came into the room, pale as snow, and said,

'How long have you had this?'

'Had what?' Louis said.

'How long have you had these symptoms?'

'Couple of weeks,' Louis said. 'Why?'

She showed him the scan. There was a tumour in his head the size of a billiard ball.

'I don't know how you're still walking around. Sit down. I'll call an ambulance.'

While they waited for it to arrive, she demanded his licence.

54

'That means I can't drive any more?'

'You can apply to get it back at a later date.'

He never did. Never got it. Never applied.

By the time I got there, Louis had already been operated on and was back out of hospital. He didn't want me to drive the ute at first as he said I had gone soft and had become effete and soft-handed due to having driven nothing but automatics for the past ten years.

'Louis,' I said. 'It's like a bicycle and an elephant – you never forget.'

'When have you ever ridden an elephant?'

'As a matter of fact—'

'You'd better hire a car,' he said. But by then pride and stubbornness had got the better of me.

I spent a morning on the phone and sorted out insurance. Then I got the keys and started up the ute. Ear-plugs would have been useful, as would a window that stayed up. But the gears were nowhere near as bad as Louis had made out. I crashed them a few times and maybe drove the wrong way up a couple of one-way streets, but once I'd got over that, we were fine.

For all that Louis' short-term memory was giving him problems, he still had a map of the city fixed in his mind, and he knew the way to Fried Fish with his eyes closed.

'Okay. Left here now,' he'd say. But then he'd raise his right hand.

Or it would be the other way around.

'It's right at this next junction coming up.'

And he'd point left.

I decided that it was the gestures that were accurate and

the words that were wrong, and so it proved to be. When he said left, I turned right.

'That's fine now. Just keep going straight on ahead here and follow the car behind you.'

'Louis—'

'What?'

'Nothing.'

I knew what he meant so I kept my mouth shut and we kept going on our way to Fried Fish. We sat outside the restaurant, with Louis in his beanie hat, smiling serenely like the Buddha, and Derek pouring the drinks out, and Babs looking kind and comfortable, and Meg, who was maybe eighty-three, looking cryptic, and Halley being genially sarcastic whenever Derek expressed a political opinion. And the afternoon passed, and everyone kept talking to Louis, even when the conversation wandered and he could follow it no longer, trying to keep him included.

But he just sat there, more Buddha-like with each passing minute and with the slow declining of the sun.

'So you're back at radiotherapy tomorrow, Louis?' Babs said.

He gave her the milky-eyed look, and there was the usual moment of suspense when you wondered, has he heard, will he answer, then he nodded and said, 'That's right, Babs. First thing tomorrow.'

'Then that's good, Louis,' she said. 'And we'll all be thinking of you.'

And he gave her the Buddha smile, peering out from under the beanie hat.

'Thank you, Babs,' he said. 'That will be nice.'

'We'll be thinking of you, fella,' Derek said. He had large hands, like garden forks, the kind of things you might use when repotting.

I looked at Louis and shared a glance with him. They were nice people, but they didn't know about the long-ago, nor the day I had come home to find Louis waiting for me in the back garden to tell me the bad news. And I didn't know about their long-agos, and that's the way the world is. You meet on the open ground somewhere, round at Fried Fish or somewhere similar, out in the sunlight. But your dark cave of memory is your own. And even if you once shared that cave with someone, they don't always seem to remember the same paintings on the walls.

'Louis,' I said to him once, 'our childhood was the most miserable thing, wasn't it, though? I used to go to sleep praying I wouldn't wake up again. And I was only ten.'

He looked at me with incredulity and hurt bewilderment.

'It wasn't that bad,' he said. 'There were a lot of good things there. Apart from the soup.'

The past isn't just a foreign country, it's a place we see different parts of. Louis had gone and looked at places there I hadn't even known existed.

8

MATADORS

Iona didn't take too warmly to news of the sun-kissed blonde from New Zealand by way of the Black Mountains. And she hadn't even met her yet. I think it was the *sun-kissed blonde* part she took exception to, as if to ask what was wrong with red-headed Celts with freckles? She and Louis had clashed before, like when he said to her, 'Your sense of humour underwhelms me,' and as a consequence I got it in the neck.

'What does he mean, my sense of humour underwhelms him?'

'Iona – I don't know.'

'Well, he's your brother.'

'It's just the kind of thing he says. Don't take it seriously.'

'Was he trying to be funny?'

'What about?'

'Was he trying to be funny about my sense of humour?'

'Iona—'

I think she had it in for him after that, at least for a while until she forgot about it and something else came along instead.

'So is he going to bring this so-called sun-kissed blonde back here like he did with the other one and have sex on the sofa while we've got to listen through the wall?'

'It was a one-off,' I said.

'It was a one-off that went on all night,' she said. 'How come he doesn't stay on his boat?'

'He's only got a small mattress,' I said.

'I expect they'll want breakfast too.'

'We can spare two bits of toast.'

Sure enough, Louis turned up with the sun-kissed blonde and they gave the sofa a good pounding.

The sun-kissed blonde was used to equestrian living and wide-open spaces, and terraced houses and small flats seemed quite a novelty.

'Look at the funny little houses, Louis,' she'd say. 'Aren't they small?'

I don't know what women saw in Louis but they must have seen something invisible to my eye. It was only towards the end that he got lonely and the lonelier he got and the more straggly his beard became and the more the dust piled up on the carpet, the harder it became to start anew.

Back before Louis and I fell out with God, we were altar boys three and a half times a week. (On average.) Three times on a Sunday we had to drag ourselves up the hill to church: for high mass at eleven, back for altar-boy tuition at three, back again for benediction at six thirty. And then every Saturday we would take it in turns to be the servers at early-morning mass.

Looking back I realise our parents probably sent us to become altar boys not merely from a sense of devotion but to get a break from us and maybe to have sex undisturbed on a Sunday afternoon.

One Saturday, a few weeks after our father's funeral, it was my turn for the six thirty Saturday rising and the bitter solo trek up the hill to put on the red cassock and the white cotta and do the honours at an ill-attended morning mass, to which only fanatics and the elderly came.

Afterwards, as I left the church, a man stopped me. He was a stranger to me and I had been warned about such and had no intention of going anywhere with him. But that wasn't what he had in mind.

'Hey, son,' he said. 'Your mother's the widow, isn't she?'

Inside I was angry, ashamed and somewhat offended at hearing my mother so described but was unable to argue with the truth of the statement. I think that those who attempt to deal with the effect of familial death upon children and the young constantly overlook one essential aspect of it all – the sheer embarrassment.

'I don't know,' I said. As I couldn't deny it, I feigned ignorance.

'Look, things can't be easy. You see she gets this.'

And the unknown man, who knew all about us, but whom I did not know, pressed some folded banknotes upon me.

'You give that to your mother, all right?'

I stared at him, uncertain what to do.

'You go straight home now and give that to your mother, okay?'

I nodded, but I did not thank him. And then he was gone and I was alone in the street with the banknotes in my hand.

A sudden excitement came into me. I was going to hurry home now, the bringer of joy and glad tidings. I would place the money upon the table and see our mother's face, at first clouded with perplexity and distrust, but then lightening with belief and with doubt dispelled as she reached out and took the notes in her hand and realised that for a brief while things would be easier and we were saved.

And it wouldn't be just her. Louis too would be amazed by my ability to go out single-handed into the world and to attract good fortune, just like that, when left to my own devices.

So I turned for home. I was anxious to keep the money safe. But along with that, I had a hankering for a certain kind of style which I had seen in films in the cinema, where men would reach into their inside pockets and take out wallets, or flat gold cigarette cases, or small guns with which to shoot their enemies.

I didn't have a coat with an inside pocket. So I stuffed the money inside my pullover and walked quickly home. It was a twenty to twenty-five minute walk.

As I entered the house, I called to my mother.

'I came out of the church,' I told her, 'and there was a man—'

Her fear changed to interest to anticipation as I described what had occurred.

'Then let's see it,' she said. 'Let me see it.'

I reached to my imaginary inside pocket, under my pullover, and, you've guessed it, the money had gone.

Her dismay was palpable, and I felt an inner sickness. To have come home with hope and then to have destroyed it was worse than coming home with nothing at all.

'It's gone. It was there. It's gone.'

I ran out and realised they were both behind me, and we scoured the street, all the way up to the church and back. But the money had gone.

I don't know if she ever believed that the money had really been there, or if the incident was but a product of a child's imagination: that aspect of it that dreams of fixing everything for the helpless, hopeless adult world – the child as hero, feted and applauded, saving the day.

She never mentioned it again. And Louis just looked at me as if I was either a liar or a thief, and he couldn't decide which, but whichever it was, I was letting the side down.

I never saw the man again either, but I would think of him, and how he must have felt as he walked away from handing me those banknotes, feeling that he had done a generous and a decent thing that would make someone else's life easier for a while. He must have been some acquaintance of my father's. He should have given the banknotes to Louis. Louis would never have lost them. But it had been Louis' turn to stay in bed that Saturday. But then again, had it been Louis' turn, maybe he would never have attracted the good fortune, so we were stymied anyway.

We carried on without the money. Its difference would have been transient and temporary. Maybe that was when I started falling out with God. I just came home from the church one morning and told my mother I wasn't going any more. She didn't try to make me, just asked me if I was sure, and I said I was. She said it was our father's idea for us to become altar boys and to have to go to church three times a day on a Sunday.

Louis kept on going and said I was letting the side down again. And then there was his brief dalliance with the possibility of the priesthood. But after he came to his senses, he stopped going to church and fell out with God too, although our mother hung on to Him, right to the end. But even there, it wasn't God so much as the fact that all her friends and acquaintances were there, all regular attenders, and without at least the simulacrum of belief, she would have had no social life and have been even lonelier than she was.

It wasn't so much God I had the trouble with, as the people who purported to act on His behalf, and who gave Him such a bad name.

'You remember that, Louis?' I asked, as I looked across the table at him.

We were drinking flat whites and sitting underneath the burners at the café run by the Malaysian girls. Louis was sitting there, looking dapper and neat with his freshly trimmed beard and cropped hair and eyebrows. He had pulled off the beanie hat as the gas burners were roasting him now.

'Don't,' he said. 'Don't.'

But I carried on reminiscing.

'You remember the soup, do you, Louis?' I said. 'You remember Mum's soup? Every Sunday, when we were back from the altar-boy training, and before we had to go off again to benediction. We'd have dinner, remember? Soup made out of mutton bones, and you had to eat it quick before the fat congealed on the top of the soup there. You remember?'

'Don't,' Louis said. 'Please don't.'

But I was remorseless.

'And then mutton for mains, and then tinned fruit and condensed milk for pudding.'

'Don't,' Louis said. 'It's too painful.'

'Happy days, eh, Louis?' I said.

'You're a bastard,' he told me.

'Come on, Louis. And do you remember, after benediction, how we'd go round to the Perkins' house, as we didn't have a TV, and they'd let us watch it, and Mum would keep jam sandwiches in her handbag for us to eat on the way home.'

'No,' Louis said. 'No more now. It was bad enough the first time round.'

'You remember their son, he was in your class. What was it he drank again? Arsenic?'

'Cyanide,' Louis said. 'He did chemistry, same as me. But he was a geek and a nerd and he didn't get on with anyone, so he got cyanide out the lab, stopped the lift between floors, and drank it.'

'His brother was nuts too, wasn't he? He'd be there at the weekends, on day release from the asylum.'

'They lived just down the road from the prison,' Louis remembered.

'That's right. They did.'

'Why were they all weird?' Louis said.

'Why were all who weird?'

'All our parents' friends. All weird or outcasts or crippled or screwed up or they had pieces missing. You remember that couple of friends of theirs? He had a calliper on his leg and she had a bad eye that looked at you sideways. All their friends were like that. They all had something wrong with them.'

'Maybe everyone's got something wrong with them.'

'No,' Louis said. 'Not seriously wrong, not like that. We had more than our fair share of crazy people and mental cases. And what about the lodgers?'

'Louis, no one who takes in lodgers expects them to be normal.'

'I want to forget all about it,' he said. 'I want to forget I ever had a childhood. But instead I remember everything. I just can't recall what happened five minutes ago.'

'We were sitting in the barber's, Louis, getting your eyebrows trimmed.'

'You want something to eat? I'm hungry.'

'Okay. Let's get some lunch. You want to see the menu?'

'I won't be able to read it.'

'I'll read it out to you.'

'And the prices.'

'Louis, you don't need to care about the prices.'

'Oh? Why not?'

'I mean we can afford it. I'll pay.'

'I'll pay. You've flown all the way over here.'

'It doesn't matter.'

'I'll pay.'

I read out the menu to him and I knocked five dollars off everything.

'Seems pricey to me,' he said – even with the five dollars deducted.

'Louis, you're all right for money, believe me, you don't need to worry.'

'They'll never give me any.'

'Louis, I talked to the hospital social worker, to Leonora. She's dealing with it. It's all going through. You'll get the money. No one expects someone with a diagnosed brain tumour to clock in on a Monday morning.'

'You don't know how it works over here. They'll find a way to wriggle out of it. We're screwed.'

'Louis—'

'I'll have a melted cheese panini.'

'Yeah, okay. Me too.'

I motioned to the waitress, who came over and took our food orders. We sat there, under the burner, in the cool, crisp Australian winter. The light was high and bright and the cars moved along the streets and the pedestrians passed us, and no one knew or cared or would ever have recognised that a condemned man and his brother sat at that table and upon those chairs. Same as I had walked past many a dying person in my time and had evinced no interest.

Louis pulled his beanie back on and sat with his Buddha smile and milky eyes, watching the world go about its business.

'You start the radiotherapy in the morning? Is that right?'

'Radio and chemo, both.'

'I read about a guy on the internet, had the same as you,

diagnosed with it seven years ago, still going. In remission and still going. Seven years.'

'That's good,' Louis said. 'That's good.'

Any port in a storm. Any straw in the wind.

The paninis arrived and we ate them hot.

'Okay, Louis?'

'This is good,' he said, cheese dribbling down his chin. That was Louis for you. Never a stylish eater. More of a hungry man with an appetite who needed to get fed.

Half way through the panini, he paused and looked across the table.

'You know something,' he said. 'You're all I've got.'

Which I thought was pretty terrible.

'Then you're in a worse way than we thought, Louis,' I said. 'It's more serious than we imagined.'

Which he had the decency to laugh at. But it made me sad. I shouldn't have been all he had. He should have had a lover still, a wife, a daughter, a son. But he'd never had children though he could have done. Chancelle would have had his babies for starters – and I doubt she was the only one.

'I could never have dealt with it,' he said to me once. 'Don't know how you coped with them. I could never have coped.'

'Louis, you don't get it. No one can cope. No one has children thinking they know what to do. It's just one generation of hopeless cases bringing up another. Nobody knows what they're doing.'

'They'd have driven me nuts.'

'Mine drive me nuts. Everyone's kids drive them nuts.'

'I'd have had a breakdown.'

'Everyone's having a breakdown. People who don't have kids have breakdowns.'

'True enough.'

'But you've got your friends.'

'I suppose so.'

'It's not like you're on your own.'

'No – maybe not.'

The next morning I woke at five to hear Louis moving about in the kitchen. The morning was chilly and I got reluctantly out of bed. Louis was standing by the table with a glass of water in his hand, wearing a paint-stained T-shirt and the sort of underpants that went out of fashion a long time since and which I didn't even know you could still buy.

'You all right?'

'Just taking my anti-nausea.'

'At this time?'

'Got to take it an hour before the chemo tablet. And then wait another hour. And then the hospital car'll come. And then go in for the radio treatment, then after that I can eat.'

'Want me to make you a sandwich to take?'

'I'm going back to bed.'

He went back to bed, resetting his alarm. I made a sandwich and left it on the table, wrapped up. Then I went back to bed too and fell asleep again.

I woke to the sound of the doorbell ringing. Louis was dressed and throwing his stuff into his cooler bag and getting ready to go.

'I'll see you later.'

'Good luck, Louis.'

The door was open now and the hospital car driver was out on the veranda at the top of the step.

'I'll see you later, Louis.'

I put my arm around him and to my surprise he kissed me. His moustache tickled and his beard was damp. I felt a moment of revulsion – to my shame. But then I wished him luck once more, and he was gone.

I wondered if the car driver realised we were brothers. We didn't look a whole lot like each other now, not with Louis travelling incognito in his beanie hat. Maybe the driver thought we were lovers instead – a couple of ageing civil partners.

I heard the car drive off and felt I should have gone too. I felt like a non-combatant who hasn't been drafted into the army yet, seeing a relative off to war. But against that was the knowledge that one day, somewhere along the road, my conscription papers would also come.

I made some coffee and sat at the kitchen table to drink it. When I had showered and dressed, I started in on Louis' paperwork. There were drawers of the stuff. I didn't really know where to begin. I dumped a load of it down on the floor.

'Louis,' I thought, 'why did you do this to me?'

Though he hadn't done anything, of course. I was just being a selfish bastard.

But aren't we all?

When our father was dying, our mother was tending to him. He was high on morphine at the time, and she said to him,

'What do you want the boys to be, John, when they grow up?'

He thought a moment and said, 'Matadors.'

Neither Louis nor I ever became a matador. There was no tradition of bullfighting round where we lived. So, in that sense, we let him down. We were actually un-acquainted with his wishes as our mother did not disclose them to us for some years, and by then it was too late to take the matadoring route. I wouldn't have done it anyway, as I lacked the courage and my reactions were no way quick enough and I didn't have a cape.

But Louis' eyes lit up when he heard about it, and he seemed to be dreaming of going to Spain. Maybe he should have done something about it. He might have been good at it. It's a cruel sport but wasn't really consid-ered so then. You could still be an elegant hero back then in a gold brocade suit with a sharp waistcoat and a stylish hat.

But I don't go for the alternative universe theory. There are too many options. How can there be other worlds for every infinitesimal variation that there could have been in our lives? That we turned right instead of left? That we crossed the road a moment earlier, a moment later? That the seats in the theatre were upholstered in red and not in blue? And this must be so for every creature that ever lived and every blade of grass and every ant that ever crawled along a leaf – but could have crawled across another leaf, in a different direction.

Where is there the space for all this infinity?

Or maybe I'm wrong and there is a world in which Louis is still driving his ute down to the harbour to potter around on his sailboat. Maybe there is a world in which he does not suffer a mysterious nausea and a sudden migraine. It's not this world though. And this is the one we must deal with.

9

STRAWBERRIES

After a while the Australian winter turned to spring. But I'd started seeing darkness and the end of things everywhere, even in the faces of children and babies sitting in prams. I'd see infants with their mothers and think why have they done it, why did they bring these people into the world only to have to die.

Finality would be there too, in old sepia memories, on the walls of restaurants and bars and hospital receptions – photographs of pioneers and illustrious founders and settlers of untamed lands. All gone and all dead, every single one of them. And if one of the men had a moustache, then so they all did; and if one of the women wore a bonnet and an impeccable white apron, the rest did too. And they were all dead.

And the waitress at Kangaroo Point would bring over

my coffee, and for all her youth and beauty, she would one day be dead. And the runners and the joggers and the personal trainers and all the pursuers of life and health and immortality, they would, without exception, all soon die.

Yet had you said to any one of them that your relative was dying, they'd have given you their sympathy, or maybe acted shocked and surprised, as if this were some uncommon event, instead of a regular and perpetual occurrence. For people are dying everywhere, every moment of the day, in their thousands and then in their millions and then in their billions too. And of the population of the world, of the eight billion or however many there are, plus those born since you began to read this sentence, one day they will all be dead, every one. And you and me and every single thing that lives, all dead. And I sat with my coffee, watching the boats on the river and the ferries taking the commuters to work, and it would all pass and be over and ended too.

And I thought that of that eight billion or more, many millions, maybe many billions believe there is another world of some spiritual kind that they will go to when they stop breathing. But I didn't think so.

'No one knows why we're here, do they, Louis?' I said to him later. 'Not even the best brains. People believe things, but faith isn't knowing. Nobody knows what we're doing here and they never will. We'll go on dying until the world falls into the sun, and we'll still never know. And that's it. People can build you an aeroplane and send men to the moon but they can't tell you what we're doing here.'

'What's for dinner?' Louis said.

'What do you want?' I said.

'Whatever you're making,' he said.

'How about egg and chips and peas, followed by straw-berries and yoghurt?'

'Man, you know how to live.'

'No need to be sarcastic.'

'I wasn't.'

'Louis, when did you last eat strawberries?'

'I don't buy them.'

'Why not?'

'They're pricey.'

'Louis, I know how much you have in the bank.'

'That's got to last me.'

'Louis, you've got to get a new fridge here.'

'What's wrong with the fridge? Nothing wrong with the fridge. I've had the fridge a quarter of a century.'

'Louis, that's what's wrong with the fridge. And it looks even older than that.'

'I got it second-hand. But it's still got some life in it.'

'That's precisely what's worrying me, Louis. There's life in your fridge I've never seen before. Grey, mouldy, whiskery life that there probably isn't an antidote for. And what about the half a grapefruit in there?'

'I'm going to eat it.'

'Louis, it's gone brown. Brown and green.'

'Be all right for a few more days.'

'And while we're buying you a new fridge, Louis, we may as well get a new washing machine.'

'Nothing wrong with the washing machine.'

'It doesn't work, Louis.'

'So what? Apart from that, it's fine.'

'Louis, you've got it plumbed into the rain-water collection tank, and when you start the pump up, it floods the basement.'

'A little water never did anyone any harm.'

'And then you have to stand there next to it, wearing wellingtons otherwise your feet will get wet, holding your wrist-watch in your hand and timing the cycle so you can change it manually because the auto part of your so-called automatic washing machine doesn't work.'

'Ah, but the matic part still works, doesn't it?'

'Louis, I don't even know what the matic part is.'

'Yeah, well, you were never much of a scientist, were you? You'd never even have got your Geography O level if I hadn't given you private tuition.'

'Louis, geography isn't science.'

'No, it's not brain surgery either.'

'What's that supposed to mean?'

'It means I've had brain surgery so I know what I'm talking about. And if you want to know about rocket science, I can explain that to you too.'

'You just can't remember your PIN number.'

'No, I can't! Bastard thing.'

'You just have to remember it as a time, Louis. Seven fifteen in the morning. What's that in numbers?'

'Zero seven one five.'

'You've got it.'

'What time did you say again?'

'Seven fifteen in the morning.'

'That's easy to remember.'

'Good, so you've got it now, and the machine won't keep your card again like it did.'

'Seven fifteen. I can remember that.'
'Good.'
'Ask me what my PIN number is.'
'What's your PIN number, Louis?'
'Easy. It's nineteen fifteen. One nine one five.'
'No, Louis, no. It's seven fifteen in the morning.'
'What is?'
'Your PIN number.'
'The bollocks it is!'
'No, it is, Louis, it is.'
'A.m.?'
'Yes, a.m., not p.m.'
'Okay. I've got it now. Let's try again.'
'Let's let a moment go past first.'
'Okay.'
'You remember what we're having for dinner?'
'Yeah. Yoghurt and chips. That right?'
'Pretty close. Okay. Let's try the PIN number again.'
'You know that strictly speaking it should just be PIN without saying number after. Because P.I.N. stands for personal identification number. So if you add another number after that, what you're really saying is personal identification number number.'
'Is that so?'
'Now, that's the kind of stuff I can remember.'
'Useful.'
'It's all the – bits and pieces – I forget.'
'Okay. Shall we try the PIN number again.'
'Just PIN. No number. Just PIN.'
'Okay. Shall we try your PIN again?'
'Okay. Shall I go first?'

'Yes, of course, Louis. There's no point in my telling you what it is. That's not going to help.'

'Okay, I'll go first with the – the bits and pieces—'

'PIN number.'

'PIN. Just PIN.'

'Okay, Louis. What's your PIN? Can you remember the mnemonic?'

'The what?'

'The *aide memoire*?'

'What *aide memoire*?'

'The little tip for remembering. The time.'

'Oh, yeah. Right. Seven fifteen. In the morning.'

'Good, good. That's great. That's progress, Louis. That's great. So what's your PIN?'

'It's – it's seven one five.'

'It's four digits, Louis, four.'

'It's – seven one five – ah, damn it!'

'Slowly, Louis, take it slowly, don't get angry. It'll come to you. There's no pressure. Just relax.'

'Zero seven one – five.'

'Got it. Perfect. See. Said you'd get it. Good. All right.'

'We're screwed, you know. We're screwed.'

'Louis, we're not screwed. You've had the surgery, they've taken out as much of the tumour as they can. Now they're going to nuke the rest and kill it with the chemo. In six months' time you can fly over and see us. We'll take a trip, go to Scotland, wherever you want to go.'

'You remember the last time I came over and we went to the book festival and saw that woman talking about that guy, whatshisname?'

'Yes, I remember.'

'We had some good times, didn't we?'

'Yes, we did, Louis. We did.'

'She talked about her life in New York and the bits and pieces. She was from that rich family.'

'Rothschild.'

'And he was that jazz player.'

'Was it Monk?'

'Yeah.'

'I'm going to start cooking in a minute, Louis. Why don't you go and watch "Deal Or No Deal"? You like that.'

'They have some right dills, on that programme. Some complete stiffs. If they just bothered to work out the mathematical odds in advance—'

'Well, you sit down and work them out.'

'Yoghurt and chips, right?'

'Kind of, yeah.'

'I'm going to lie down a while.'

'Don't fall asleep.'

'What's my PIN number?'

'You tell me.'

'Zero seven – one – eight.'

'Fifteen, Louis. Seven fifteen.'

'Zero seven one five, damn it. I'm so stupid. I'm so stupid. I'm just so goddamn stupid.'

'Louis, you are not stupid. You were always cleverer than the rest of us put together.'

'It's the bits and pieces. The damn – bits and pieces . . .'

'I know, Louis. I know. I'm going to start cooking now.'

'Okay. Hey. Zero seven one three! That's it, isn't it. Zero seven one three.'

'You're getting better all the time, Louis. But let's leave

the PIN for now. Let's have a rest from it. We can come back to it later. That's the secret. Not too much at once.'

'I'm going to watch "Deal Or No Deal".'

'I'll call you when it's ready.'

'Hey – what's that? Did you buy some strawberries?'

'We got them in the supermarket earlier.'

'You know how to live, huh. You know how to live.'

'I'll call you when it's ready.'

And he went to watch TV.

But I've got it in me now and it won't go away. Other people celebrate the new-born baby and the lamb in the field. I just think the beautiful creature is going to die, and how we were all once like that – the welcomed arrival, the treasured child, the celebrated birth, the golden infant to do wonders in the world. And look what happened. We grew up into Louis and me. We grew up into men with beer bellies and women of hard experience and of lost and regretted youth. We grew to become the crowds in the subway and the tired, weary faces on the trains. Which is really no way to think about things.

No good way at all. But maybe it will pass.

10

CAT

The sun-kissed blonde was called Bella, and while I felt Louis had maybe exaggerated about the sun-kissed part – for the UK weather was not helping in that respect, and her tan faded even as you looked at her – she seemed presentable enough and not lacking in charm, even if most of that charm did not work on others the way it worked on Louis.

It is normally the colonisers who think the natives quaint. But time had changed all this for Bella and things were on the other foot. We were a land of those who did things differently, for lack of knowledge of how to do them properly, and who lived in peculiar houses with inferior plumbing and nowhere to keep the horses.

But she and Louis got along, and if love had a passport photograph of what it looked like, it maybe looked like the two of them back then. It wouldn't look like that now. It got barely recognisable. But then time does that to most IDs.

Bella was only seeing the old world, and not intending to adopt it as a permanent residence – what with the inconveniences of it and the lack of decent stabling facilities in town.

All the same, she put up with our sofa for a while, to Iona's irritation, which soon became so obvious that they moved out and found a place of their own, and shortly afterwards Louis announced that he was going south with her, to live in Australia and start a whole new career. Which I thought something of a misnomer, as Louis hadn't yet had an old career, so it was premature to be thinking of a new one already.

They packed their bags and took a slow boat, calling in at interesting places along the way. International phone calls were still expensive and postcards were a lot of trouble, and Louis was never big on them anyhow, so we lost touch a little and he drifted on with his life and I went on with mine.

Iona went off to have someone else's babies and left me with her cat, Henry. Henry had been in poor mental condition almost since the day he had been born, for his mother had been guillotined by a collapsing window, the sash cord of which had perished and which had been propped open for ventilation with an unreliable stick.

The stick gave way while Henry's mother was under the heavy window frame, down it came, and that was the start of Henry's bereaved and traumatised mental troubles. Maybe he suffered from separation anxiety, maybe he just didn't like the food I gave him, but he seemed to go out of his way to annoy me, howling to get out in the middle of the night and then, the instant I had returned to bed, howling to get in again. I installed a cat flap, but he preferred the howling arrangement. And then when I was thawing some mince out on top of the fridge, back in my carnivorous days, I discovered him with his face in it, polishing off what was going to be an essential ingredient in my spaghetti bolognese.

To my shame I chased him around the garden, throwing the remaining mince at him, shouting, 'You want some mince? Here, have this!', while the curtains twitched in adjacent properties and summary judgements were made behind them.

And then, going on a holiday, I had to put him in a cattery for a week. I knew he didn't like the place from the moment we arrived and he refused to get out of the box without extensive cajoling and much persuading. When I got back from holiday, he wouldn't speak to me, not even in a feline way. He turned his back on me and plainly bore an eternal grudge now and things were never the same, not even when he got tape worms and I cleared up the mess and bought his tablets from the vet and made sure that he took them and got him treats.

I think he wanted to be with Iona and maybe felt twice abandoned, once by his mother, whom the window had done for, and then by Iona, whom the urge to have babies had done for. I resented her leaving us quite a lot too, for she had gone off to have babies with someone we would never have met if it hadn't been for Louis – for Nigel was one of Louis' dock-side friends. That was typical of Louis,

I thought, that he should introduce some acquaintance of his into our lives who would then disappear with my girlfriend to have babies. And instead of accepting responsibility for the situation, Louis then simply disappeared himself, off to the Antipodes with sun-kissed blondes, leaving me on my own in a rough part of town with no mince and a disturbed cat with worms.

There were occasions when resentment got the better of me and I fell to brooding. To my mind, it had all been about Louis our whole lives. Since I was small I had been told by our parents of the greatness of Louis and the ambitions there were on his behalf. Louis was to go to a good school, and then to university – the first in the clan ever to do so – and then the oystered world out there would be waiting for his selection and his prising open, and he could take the one he wanted.

Louis and our widowed mother would pass hours together in the kitchen discussing the glories of his future, of what he should aim for, of whether he was an Oxford man, or if Cambridge might suit him better, or whether Harvard was more the place.

One afternoon, home from school, listening again to my mother describe to me the glory of Louis' prospects and the extent of his current attainments – for he was first in his class in everything, always – I said to her, just out of casual, if not selfish, interest,

'And what about me?'

She looked at me blankly, as if this were either an irrelevant question or simply one that had never occurred to her.

'Oh, you'll be all right,' she finally said. 'Maybe you'll get a job as an electrician.'

And this was my mother talking to the boy who had once taken the cover off a wall switch and stuck his finger into it just to see what might happen. (I was propelled six feet across the room.)

So I realised that in my case not much was expected by way of academic achievement and, not wishing to make trouble in that case, I did my best to oblige, and took to juvenile delinquency, for which, it appeared, I had a natural aptitude and no small talent. So I took that up, along with smoking, staying out late in park shelters, and sitting in the cinema watching films I was too young for, having lied about my age to get in. I'd like to say they were happy days. But nothing's ever that simple or so uncompromised that it can legitimately bear that description without mitigating circumstances or footnotes.

In the end, Henry the cat got kidney problems and was put down and out of his misery. They don't offer that service for human beings yet, at least not in many parts of the world.

11

TRICKS

One afternoon Halley rang up, when Louis was in the hospice, and said, 'How is he? How's it going?'
I said, 'It's the same as it was, Halley. He might know I'm here but I don't know because he doesn't say anything. They come round and turn him over once every three hours and that's about it. Most of the time his eyes are closed and there's a machine for the drugs.'

'Well, look, we've got tickets for the late-night cabaret at the Spiegel Tent and were going to ask Louis along, but in the circumstances – what are you doing?'

'I suppose it wouldn't matter if I wasn't here for a few hours.'

'I'll tell you where to meet us.'

I felt I was turning into a Louis substitute – like him, but not him, yet close enough to do. Old resentments rekindled in me. I'd thought them doused, but they were merely smouldering. It was always so.

'Hey – you're Louis' brother, aren't you?'

And thus defined. Which is no good to anybody – to be defined as simply being related to somebody else. What use is that, when you want to colonise your own territory, and plant your own flag? But maybe that is the inevitable consequence of coming along later and of not having the sense to get there first.

I met Halley and another friend of Louis – Phil – in a downtown bar, sitting drinking Little Creatures, which seemed to be the bottle to buy. So I ordered the same and we downed those and then ate in Lock and Load, then headed towards the South Bank, which was teeming. There was a festival on and crowds everywhere and Chinese lanterns and dragons, and there by the river was the Spiegel Tent, with the romance of old Vienna about it, and the tantalising scent of the forbidden and of slight decay.

We went in and sat at the rear, perched on the backs of the seats, feet on the flip-downs, or we'd have been too low to get a view. The crowd was lively and most people had glasses in their hands. There were transvestites, and men and women who looked like they might have had sex changes. There was a heady decadence which made for a good and receptive atmosphere. It was getting on for midnight when the show started and there were acrobats and cabaret artistes and a lot of exposed flesh. The high spot was a woman who made small handkerchiefs vanish.

She appeared in a smart and formal business suit and

made one handkerchief disappear. Then, adopting a perplexed look, as if to say, 'Where'd it go?' she shrugged her jacket off, in case it might be hiding in there. But it wasn't.

Yet the handkerchief then reappeared in her hands, so she made it disappear again, and again the perplexed look. Was it in the waistband of her skirt perhaps? So the skirt came off.

And so it continued. Her shirt came off, her bra came off, and still those handkerchiefs went on inexplicably disappearing.

Finally, with a shall-I, shan't-I expression, followed by one conveying that having come this far she might as well, she took her pants off. Still no handkerchief, but a fine and well-shaved vagina. Then she made the handkerchief reappear, but I won't go into details.

She got a big round of applause – and no doubt deserved it.

Over a final drink afterwards, Halley said,

'Louis would have enjoyed that.'

'I don't doubt it,' I told him. 'So how'd she do it?'

But none of us knew.

When I got home I Googled 'Disappearing handkerchief trick'. I rang Halley the next day.

'She's got a false thumb,' I said.

'She's got a what?'

'A false thumb. A false thumb made out of plastic that fits over your real thumb, and you take it on and off and hide it in your fist, and that's where the handkerchief comes and goes from.'

'A false thumb?' Halley said. 'How do you know?'

'It's a standard magician's trick,' I told him. 'Taking all your clothes off is just a variation on the theme.'

'You've spoiled the mystery for me,' Halley said.

'How about the nudity?' I asked him.

'No,' he said. 'The memory of that remains intact.'

'Then you've kept the good part,' I said. 'Because if she'd just made handkerchiefs vanish but had kept her clothes on—'

'She wouldn't be doing late-night cabaret.'

'Precisely.'

'Oh well – pity Louis couldn't be there.'

'I told him about it when I got in to the hospice.'

'Did he react?'

'I don't know if he heard or understood me, but maybe in some deep recess of his mind—'

'They say your sense of hearing is the last to go.'

'That's what the nurses keep saying to me, but how would anyone know? Or is it just what they tell you, so that when you keep on talking, you don't feel such a fool?'

'So he didn't react?'

'Not really.'

'Not even when you mentioned the pants coming off?'

'No, Halley, not even then.'

'But you never know.'

'That's true.'

'Tell Louis I'll be in to see him. When are you going back round?'

'I'm there now. But I wouldn't worry, Halley, I don't think he'll know you. I don't think he knows me or anyone. I squeeze his arm or hold his hand but he doesn't respond any more.'

'Well, I might come by anyhow.'

'I'll be here.'

'Okay.'

'I might drop back to the house. But if I'm not here, I'll soon be back.'

'Okay.'

'And thanks for the ticket.'

'Louis would have enjoyed that, wouldn't he?'

'He would, Halley. He would.'

'A false thumb, eh?' he said again. 'Well, even if it was, the rest of her seemed genuine.'

'You didn't think there was a little silicone there?' I asked.

'Possibly. But well applied,' he said. 'And Louis would have liked it.'

I sat by the bedside. Louis could neither eat nor drink any more. He was unconscious all the time, his eyes like slits, curtained portholes. Every few hours the nurses came and turned him, to keep the bedsores at bay. There was a syringe driver under the bed-sheet, which kept him topped up with morphine and various other ingredients of a drug cocktail that the doctor had dispensed. If Louis moaned or groaned or reached for his head, the good nurses might give him an extra morphine shot to help him rest. He had no drip as liquid would just prolong the end. They wet his mouth with a swab, and when I said, 'Isn't he very thirsty? He's had no fluids now for days,' their answer was no, that he was all right.

But how did they know? How do you know?

I sat with him, reading books and changing the music on the CD player, his Van Morrison records and his Annie

89

Lennox and his Bach and Chet Baker and others I had never heard of, who played melancholy jazz with feeling and sang torch songs of love and loss, about good times gone, back when love was new and youth was taken for granted.

The next day I brought in photographs, because I wanted the nurses to know that Louis hadn't always been an ageing man with straggly and lost hair, and with a big scar on the side of his head, and a matted beard and wild eyebrows again – which had grown back.

I wanted them to know that he too had had youth and looks and spirit and adventures and had travelled and seen the world and had made things and done things, and women had loved him and cried over him and had wanted him for themselves.

I brought in pictures of his younger self, of him together with old lovers, on decks and beaches, on marinas and sand. I brought in a picture of the boat he sailed up the east coast for six months, he and Kirstin.

One of the nurses came in and saw the pictures, and offered to Blu-Tack them up in the window, so I thanked her and let her do it – she said it wouldn't damage them.

'We like pictures,' she said. And I thought yes, I'd hoped that.

I don't say it gets you any better treatment, though maybe in my heart and at the back of my mind I thought that the more they saw the dying man on the bed in front of them as a human being with a past and a story, the nicer they might be. Though they were all professional and compassionate. But it didn't do any harm.

I looked at the pictures and changed the music and

dozed on the spare bed in the corner. When they came to change him, I wandered to the room with the TV and coffee maker in it, and sometimes met other relatives there, same as me, in the small hours of the morning and in the long, empty afternoons. We'd talk, but didn't really say much: Where you from? Who are you sitting with? What do they have? Sorry to hear that. Thank you. And good luck to you also.

Then maybe you might not see them again.

So you wait and wait, and wait and wait. The hours become days and you lose sense of time, while the world out there goes about its necessary business, but you're looking down on it, from behind the double glazing, watching the silent dawn and deserted highway turn to bright morning and commuting throng. Then the traffic eases but stays consistent, then builds up again, then eases once more, then the darkness settles and the cars turn on their lights, then the traffic becomes sparser, like the last drops of water from a shut-off tap, just a trickle, a dribble, and then it stops, and it's late and silent again, and the highway is empty, and there is the hum of equipment and occasionally a buzzer sounds or you hear a trolley, and another day has gone, then another. Then you realise that you've been there nearly a week now, and no real change, and you wonder how much longer, not that you want to deprive those you love of useful life, but this – but this . . .

And that's all it seems like, like a thing unnecessarily prolonged, and you see the kind nurses and think, 'Please, couldn't you? Just another shot? A good, decent shot. That's all it would take.'

But they can't, because that's the law.

So everyone goes on waiting and thinks, well, not much longer now, soon, surely, soon. But being tough, that's not what Louis wants. So he hangs on in there, and we hang on with him. And none of us has a choice.

12

CROSSING

I came out of the twenty-four-hour mini-mart and joined the crowd at the lights, waiting to cross the road. I had the usual stuff in the bag: chocolate bars, crisps, cereal bars, bottles of juice, newspaper, spare toothbrush, toothpaste, that kind of thing – all the objects, necessary and unnecessary, that you carry to the hospital and put in the bedside cabinet, just in case and because you never know.

The road was a busy one, five lanes of thundering traffic, with preoccupied drivers at the wheels, thinking of deadlines and commitments and obligations; of clients who had to be visited and things that had to be done; of work and meals and children to be picked up; of marriages on the rocks; of love just lately come along, and love dying; of holiday arrangements and financial problems; of property, of rents; of mortgages; of concerts; of football games; of ideas for novels; of manuscripts dispatched and of fame and money to come.

We stood in a bunch, waiting for the green man to start flashing so that we could stream across and walk on up to the hospital. The lights took a long time to change. Over the road from us was another group of people waiting to come to where we were, as if in confirmation of the other man's grass being believed to be eternally greener and the necessity of investigating that conjecture to prove or disprove it.

Plenty of individuals had already poked the button to change the lights, but as more people came along, more of them gave it an extra prod, maybe to be on the safe side, maybe from impatience and anxiety, maybe because they thought the rest of us looked like the kind of simple-minded types who would stand at crossings indefinitely, never taking the initiative, but resigned to waiting for fate to intervene on our behalf.

I looked around as we waited and I saw that almost every other person there was the same as me – they were holding a bag from the mini-mart or clutching an armful of purchases. It was all the same stuff too, all the things that people take to those laid up in hospitals: fruit and sweet things, drinks and magazines, toiletries and tissues, small bunches of flowers.

It was all probably quite useless too, and would be dumped in a locker and never used. But there we all were anyway, doing the only thing we could think of, as we were fit for not much else.

The people around me appeared preoccupied and

stressed and strained. There were problems here that they could not solve, that the experts who specialised in such things could not solve, for there was no solution to them, despite illusions to the contrary – those great illusions of cure and scientific advancement and huge revolving machines that looked like wonders but which had reputations that no machine could ever live up to.

The people were staring ahead at the lights, some impatient, some seeming content to stand and wait, maybe not even wanting the lights to change at all – ever. If we could, some of us would have stood there in eternal waiting, knowing that things, at least, would not get worse.

I looked at all the mostly useless purchases and thought that at every crossing by every hospital in every city of the world such scenes went on. Fathers and mothers, husbands and wives, sisters and brothers, daughters and sons, lovers and neighbours and friends – and there they all stood, with their armfuls of small items, as they waited for the lights to change.

And when they finally did, everyone would hurry across the tarmac, and take the path up to the hospital entrance, and from there they would follow the corridors or ascend in the lifts, and then enter the wards and rooms, with their white and green order, with their flashing lights and their buzzers and bleeps.

They would take their places at the bedsides, moving a chair, opening a cupboard, saying a word. I got you this. I bought you some . . .

In every hospital in every city and town in every country.

I read somewhere that at any one time there are a million people in the sky, sitting in aeroplanes, being carried around the world. How many there are in hospitals, I do not know. Maybe the same, maybe more. Probably more, I would guess.

On the planes the hostesses and stewards bring the passengers their cashew nuts and drinks. On the ground people flood into hospitals, bringing whatever they got in the mini-mart down the road, which does good business, being where it is.

But it's all they can do. They have no stethoscopes or scalpels or medical expertise, so they bring their worry and love and concern and care, disguised as small packages, as lumps of confectionery and tubes of cream and toothpaste and as bottles of shampoo. It's almost like praying. It won't make any difference or really do any good, but you do it anyway, because there isn't anything else.

At last the lights changed and we went across. The crowd crossing the other way moved too, and we passed through each other with a thousand small and instinctive adjustments so that we did not clash, nor bump, nor collide, like two shoals of fishes passing through and rejoining, and somehow remaining whole. And then, once arrived on the other side of the road, we dispersed, the way that the great rivers of commuting cars turn homeward in the night time and the way the crowd becomes individual again, and each droplet of that river has its own peculiar and particular dimension and destination, and they all become human again. Each car contains a person with a life of some kind and a home of some kind to return to – even if a solitary and a lonely one. All those great floods and rivers that sweep along the magnificent highways and alongside the towers of glass and aspiration and brilliant light are reduced to their elements by their homecoming. And so were we.

We entered the hospital and some checked the boards while others already knew the wards they wanted. And we dispersed, like teams at the blowing of a whistle, or children at the ringing of a bell. Away we went, and it was just each of us now, and the strength of our numbers was gone. There was only the bag of grapes and the pack of razors and the magazine that would never be looked at and the already stale news of the newspapers to give us courage.

Then we entered our wards and found those we were there to visit, and we tried not to seem too falsely hearty, yet to carry ourselves with optimism and confidence and inner strength.

'Hi, Louis,' I said. 'I got you some chocolate bars and stuff.'

But he was asleep and didn't hear me. So I put the things in his locker, and pulled a chair up and sat by the bed. Then I turned the pages of the newspaper I had brought and listened to the sound of his breathing. The air conditioning hummed and then a buzzer sounded as someone's IV drip ran low and triggered a sensor and after a few minutes a nurse came and attached a new one and then the sound of the buzzing stopped.

13

CHAIN

Louis didn't come back. By six p.m. I wondered what had happened to him, but then I also thought that I was his brother, not his mother, and he was grown-up and could go where he wanted and do what he liked, and it was none of my business, even if a chunk of his brain had been taken out.

But eventually I rang the car service at the hospital to ask what was going on. They told me his return trip had been cancelled. I asked by whom. They didn't know, but that it probably meant he'd been kept in. So I called the main switchboard and found him on the oncology ward. He'd passed out after the radiotherapy treatment and they were keeping him in.

Louis' house was called a Queenslander, a kind of bungalow up on stilts, with outer stairs leading up to rear and side verandas and to the back and main doors.

The house was divided into two units. His ex-partner, the once sun-kissed – and now maybe a little sun-damaged – blonde still owned the front part of the house, which she no longer lived in but rented out, while Louis had the back. He and Bella hadn't been a couple in over twenty years now, but had never sorted out the house ownership and their affairs were still entangled, like inter- and over-growing tree roots.

Under the house was a storage area, with room for parking cars, keeping canoes, setting up work benches and storing tools.

Louis had a couple of bikes down there, so I took one of them and set off for the hospital. It was a twenty-minute ride away, along a cycle way and through a park.

The light was going and the air was cooling down. I rode past a flood-lit ground where school children were playing Australian Rules football, their coaches and parents shouting them to glory. Alongside the path, high up and dangling from the trees, were myriad fruit bats, hanging upside down and starting to move, now that it was twilight, in search of food.

They stank. They had a sweet, sickly smell of warm urine and rotten apples and bananas turning brown.

'If you ever need to use the bike,' Louis had said, 'there's a lock and chain and a pump and patches in the bag there.'

So I had slung it over my shoulder and taken it along. I got to the hospital and found a place to secure the bike. Then I opened the bag up and took out the lock and chain.

Sonofabitch.

It was Louis all over. It was Louis once again. It wasn't a proper bike lock at all. It was a small brass padlock and a very short length of chain with a few loops of metal to it that looked like a remnant of some longer, more useful thing.

I tried to wrap the chain around the tube of a post, but it was too short and wouldn't go round.

Sonofabitch, Louis.

I tried a drainpipe, the pipe of a traffic sign, I tried a railing, a fence.

Goddamn it, Louis.

The ends of the chain wouldn't meet. What the hell did he ever chain his bike to with a chain like this?

Goddamn it, Louis, I thought. Goddamn it and goddamn you too.

Anger and frustration welled up in me and for a while turned to rage and bitterest resentment.

Goddamn typical, Louis, just so goddamn typical.

And I kicked the bike and chucked the chain down and I thought to myself, Yeah, Louis, yeah. This is you, isn't it? This is you all over; this is you all round. This is just so goddamn typical of you and always was. Always going for the make and do, Louis, and the cheap option. Always bodging something up and going for the temporary fix. This is you all over, isn't it, Louis, with the kettle that doesn't have a handle and the water heater that breaks down and it takes you ten years to repair. And then, when you do get it fixed, the sink doesn't drain away. And the shower doesn't drain either, and you have exactly one minute to stand in it before it overflows.

This is you, isn't it, Louis? This was always you and always will be, ever since we were kids. And even back then, there you were, with your pullover tucked into your trousers, or your clashing colours, or your tie tucked into your belt, or one half of your collar stuck up, and you oblivious to it all when I was trying to be a bit cool.

And you and your goddamn telescope and the huge slabs of glass you were going to grind into lenses. You couldn't just buy them ready made. Oh no. You had to do it the hard way, make things as difficult as possible for yourself and for everybody else too. And then, when it couldn't be done, you'd get depressed about it, and give up, and then get equally as impractical about something else.

And now it's this goddamn chain, Louis, that doesn't have enough links to go around anything. This is you all over, isn't it? You've screwed me up once again.

I felt angry enough for violence and frustrated enough for tears. I wished he was fit and healthy so I could have got hold of him and had a good and decent row with him and told him the facts.

It's always been like this, hasn't it, Louis? What the hell is wrong with you? Why are you so goddamn impractical? Why do you do these crap jobs so undemanding of your capabilities, and then take them so seriously and conscientiously, and why do you want so much for everyone to give you responsibilities that they won't pay you for – except to give you some cheap cost-nothing compliment saying what a good worker you are, that you seem to treasure so much?

101

Is that it, Louis? Is that what you want? A pat on the back and a well done? Just like back at school when you were coming first in all the exams and it was, Well done, Louis, all the time. Is that all it is, just wanting that again?

And then there was your boat, Louis, your goddamn narrow boat down on the docks, that you were always going to fix up and never did. And the women you used to bring back and screw on my sofa, while Iona and I lay in bed on the other side of that cheap partition wall, hearing every embarrassing grunt and squeal of it.

And you remember that one time, do you, Louis, when you asked us to your narrow boat for Sunday lunch, and we got there at one, and at six o'clock that same evening we were still waiting for the chicken to cook on that stove you had, and you ended up boiling it. Boiled chicken and hard carrots. And then we ended up in a pub, just to take the taste away.

And then there was the house, wasn't there, Louis, that you were going to build one day. Buy the land and build a place and be self-sufficient, and all very admirable and fine. Only you weren't just going to build a house, were you, Louis, no, first of all you were going to make the goddamn bricks. That's right. Make the goddamn bricks and saw the goddamn timbers yourself in person, because that would be more authentic and in tune with the land. Maybe you even intended to plant the goddamn trees first and that was why nothing ever got done. And it never did, did it, Louis, or maybe only occasionally. For, in fairness, you did build that sailboat, the one still down there at Manly Harbour. But now, you look inside it, and there's junk everywhere and the head's off the engine and there

102

isn't even a patch of room to sit down, and everything stinks of oil and grease and damp and rot.

Goddamn it, Louis. I could hate you sometimes. The kettle with no handle and the frying pan covered in rust and the filthy cutlery and dirty plates and the five inches of dust under the bed, so thick it's turning into dread-locks, and the tacky curtains and the Salvation Army furniture with the price stickers still on it. And the oven you have to light in a special way because there's a knack to it. And the things you have to give a bang or a tap or a kick to, to get them to work. And the goddamn ute with the window that slowly falls down and the blower that's stuck on maximum and the radio that doesn't work, and the passenger door that can only be opened from the inside and all the crap, Louis, all the goddamned crap that you have always lived with your whole life for no good reason. You, with all your damned degrees and your exam passes. Why, Louis, why? And why isn't there someone here now, Louis, by your side? I mean, okay, you have some good friends, I know that. But what went wrong, Louis? Why isn't Bella here or Kirstin or Chancelle or Martha? Or a couple of grown-up children? Or a dog?

I've come half way around the world, Louis, and, of course, I'd have done that anyway. But if there had been someone else here, Louis, some woman who cared for you, some man who loved you, someone I could share this with. Not just the slightly arm's-length distance of friend-ship, but the intimacy of love, of a bed and a breakfast table shared – why is there no such person here now, Louis, what happened, where and why have they gone? They were there once. So what happened?

But no. There isn't anyone like that. And now I've cycled out here, Louis, on your goddamned bike, and the gears don't change properly, you know that, Louis? And you need to adjust the saddle. You're my height and I'm yours and the saddle is far too goddamn low. And how long have you been riding the bike like that for? How long, Louis? Yeah. That's what I thought. Exactly. Precisely, Louis. That's my point.

And your clothes, Louis. And the beard and eyebrows. And the out-at-elbow pullovers and the shorts splattered in paint and stained with oil. No, it's not the tumour, Louis, you were always like it, always. For Chrissake, Louis, for Chrissake. What about me, Louis? What about me? Why'd you never ask about me, every time you rang up or I called you over the years, why'd you never ask about me?

I couldn't find anywhere to secure the bike, so I just left it somewhere to take its chances. If it got stolen, too bad, and if it didn't, then that was lucky.

I went into the hospital and found the way to the oncology unit and went up and I discovered him there, in a room with two other guys and three other beds, one of them empty.

'Hi, Louis.' He looked drawn and tired and half-asleep. 'How are you feeling?'

A nurse came in and explained that he had passed out after the radiotherapy and they were keeping him in at least until they had done another scan; they were worried that the brain was swelling and pressing against the skull. He was on anti-inflammatories and painkillers and anti-nauseas and his chemo, and then he still had his glaucoma drops to take.

'How are you, Louis?'

He looked up and smiled and seemed pleased to see me.

'I'm okay. How are you?'

'I'm all right, man. Don't worry about me. I'm all right.'

Then I remembered the time, shortly after our father had died, when I couldn't sleep and lay staring at the moonlight in my bed in the room we shared.

'Louis,' I said. 'Are you awake?'

'Yeah,' he said. 'I'm awake.'

'Louis, tell me a story. You remember those stories Dad used to tell. Tell me one of those.'

'Okay,' he said. 'If you want.'

And I remembered his voice and the comfort of it as he made up some story using the same characters that our father had once invented – or maybe they were characters someone had told him stories about too.

And then I fell into sleep, while Louis was still telling me the story, and I'd always felt a little bad about that – as I'd requested the story in the first place, but hadn't stayed awake enough to hear it all.

Louis, I thought, goddamn it, Louis. It's not your fault or mine or anyone's. It's just how it is and how people are, and how the world is, and no one can do anything about it.

'You want a cup of tea or something, Louis? Can I get you something?'

'Yeah, cup of tea, thanks.'

There was a small kitchen area for the use of visitors. I made some tea for us. While I did a nurse came along and started talking to me and asked who I was visiting. Then, out of the blue, she said,

'And does he have a funeral plan?'

There was almost malice in her voice.

'You what?' I said.

'Funerals can be expensive,' she said. 'Your brother got a funeral plan?'

I looked at her. What I wanted to say to her was, Are you sick? Do you think I give a shit whether my brother has a funeral plan? Do you think I wouldn't pay to bury my own brother?

I walked away, disgusted, and took the tea to the ward.

She was the only one. Everyone else was kindness itself. But maybe there always has to be someone like that, just to keep you on your toes.

Louis managed to sit up and drink his tea.

'How'd you get here?' he said. 'Did you walk? Drive?'

'No,' I said. 'I was worried about driving. I borrowed your bike and cycled.'

'Did you remember where I told you the bag was, with the puncture repair kit and the lock and everything?'

'Yeah, I remembered.'

'That was all okay then?'

'Yeah, it was fine, Louis. It was fine.'

14

JACK AND MAY

Louis used to house-sit for a couple of people who were elderly but laden and who liked to travel. He just seemed to let himself be taken advantage of, or that was how it appeared to me. But, plainly, he didn't see it that way.

Louis, could you just . . .?

Yeah, sure thing.

Louis, would you mind?

That's no problem.

They had a nice house, a swimming pool, antique furniture and cats. Louis would keep an eye on the place for them – go round after a long day's work, pick up the mail, feed the cats, come back the next morning, feed the cats again. They invited him to dinner once in a while and that was it.

Louis, we know it's Christmas coming up but would you mind?

Louis, we hope it isn't too inconvenient, but you're such a good friend . . .

They went quiet when the tumour arrived. They went to ground, like the enemy was coming.

'It's strange I've not heard from Jack and May,' Louis told me. 'Maybe I ought to ring.'

He could barely dial a number straight by then.

'What's the bits and pieces again?' he said.

'The number? You want me to ring them?'

'Okay.'

So I did and left messages telling them he had this thing growing in his head. After a couple of weeks they got round to ringing back.

'We are so sorry to hear of your troubles, so sorry, Louis. Why don't you come over and bring your brother round to see us?'

No question that they might head in the opposite direction and come over to see him.

'Shall we go round to see Jack and May?'

'If you want to, Louis.'

'I'll take you round to see them.'

So we went in the ute, with Louis sitting in the passenger seat, giving the customary directions, such as 'Turn left at that last corner,' and 'Stop at the green light.'

Jack and May lived in a kind of faded splendour, with an unplayed piano in their huge sitting room, with Turkish carpets on the floor and soft, sinking sofas in chintz and silk coverings, deep in cushions.

'Louis, how are you, and how nice to meet your family. You'll have a drink, of course?'

It was quarter to three in the afternoon and May was already on the chilled white and Jack wasn't far behind her.

'Can't drink any more, because of the tumour,' Louis said.

'And I'm driving.'

She made us tea and proffered a plate of biscuits and a brittle chocolate confection called Rocky Road.

'I made it myself. Louis loves my Rocky Road, don't you?'

'It's very nice, May.'

'I always give him some to take back home. I'm going to give you this when you go.'

We sat and made small talk, or rather, to be more truthful, we listened to theirs. They had a litany of anecdotes concerning themselves and their travels and Jack's considerable successes as an amateur actor.

'I was once offered the opportunity to go professional. But I have no regrets, no regrets.'

I don't know why it is but whenever people start reassuring you that they have no regrets it always seems like an admission of the opposite.

May was like a faded beauty of some kind, from a Tennessee Williams play, only with an Australian flavour. She dressed in flowing pastel shades and wore significant jewellery, and the rings on her hands clinked against the crystal of her wine glass, which she refilled often.

Most of her travelling anecdotes involved situations and

circumstances in which she was forced to seek shelter and sanctuary upon premises where alcohol was served.

'So we were in New York, weren't we, Jackie, and the weather was so vile, so vile, so cold. Well, I thought I was just going to freeze, and so I said to you, didn't I, Jackie, I've just got to go in here and get something to warm me up or I'm simply going to die.'

'That's right, May.'

'But he had some gallery to go to, so I said, Well, you can go there without me.'

'I said I'd join you later.'

'So I went into this place and I said, Gentlemen, I am just so cold here in your city. We live in warm places and I'm not used to it, so what do you suggest for a warming cup? And the man at the bar there, he said, Lady, you want to try one of these. So I said, I'll have the same as this gentleman's having.'

'Bourbon, May. It was bourbon.'

'Well, whatever it was, it worked. It warmed me up nicely, so I just stayed there and kept warm until Jackie found me.'

'That's right, May.'

'And by then it was even colder outside, and so I said, Well, you can do what you like, Jackie, but I am staying here. And so I did.'

'You did, May. We did.'

'And then, Jackie, if I may interrupt you for just one second, there was that time in Bath. Do you know Bath, maybe? Louis said you lived near Bath? You do? Well, you'll know it then. Very Georgian, that's right, with the Roman Baths. But the rain. The rain! And I said to Jackie,

I said, Jackie, I simply cannot stay out in this weather. I simply cannot. I just have to get inside to get dry. And fortunately – fortunately – we were walking past a very nice, very English, very friendly – it was a hostelry. That's right. And I said, Jackie, you can go and look at all the architecture you like, but right now I need something to keep me dry. So I left him to his own devices.'

'I said I'd see you later.'

'That's right. He said he'd see me later and abandoned me to my fate, and so I went into this hostelry and I could have been raped or mugged or God knows—'

'May—'

'Well, for all I knew I was taking my life in my hands.'

'May, it was slap bang in the middle of town, about twenty steps from the Roman Baths—'

'Well, I wasn't to know that, I could hardly see the pavement under my feet with all the rain. And my shoes, well – soaking. I should have had Wellington boots. So I left Jackie to whatever it is he gets up to when he goes off on his own—'

'May, I didn't go off. It was you who went off. We were heading for the museum—'

'And so I went in and I said, Gentlemen, I am so soaked through. I cannot believe the weather you have here. Now, what on earth would you suggest that a visitor to these climes ought to have to keep her dry when the rain's coming down like this? So a gentleman at the bar, he said—'

'It was white wine, May.'

'It was not white wine, it was no such thing.'

'That was what you were drinking when—'

'Well, you didn't turn up again for hours.'

'No, but I—'

'So anyway, Louis, how are you? And how sad to hear about this tumour. But you're going to be all right. They can do such marvellous things now – marvellous things. Well, I'm going to have one more drink before tea time so why don't we all do the same? Oh no, you can't, can you? Then how about your brother? Oh, he's driving. But he could have one? No? Just one?'

'May, don't force him—'

'I am not forcing him, Jackie, not forcing him. I have never ever forced anyone to have any kind of drink of any kind, I am merely being hospitable. Hospitable. And making people welcome.'

So she filled up her glass and Jackie's glass too.

'Well, Louis dear, before your brother goes home you must both come round and eat some dinner, mustn't they, Jackie? Mustn't they?'

'Well, if Louis is up to it.'

'Of course he's up to it, look at him, he's like an ox, and you've had your beard trimmed, haven't you, Louis?'

'We went to the barber's.'

'I thought you had.'

'I think we ought to go now,' Louis said.

'But you've only—'

'Louis gets very tired, very quickly, it's the radiation treatment and all the drugs.'

'Of course, of course. Well, let's make it next week, next Tuesday. And you take the Rocky Road with you. You take the Rocky Road, Louis, as I know you like it and I can always make some more.'

So we left with a bag of Rocky Road and they saw us out to the ute. A blind cat watched us leave – or, at least, its head pointed in our exiting direction.

'Do you think this is a good idea, Louis?' I asked him as we drove away. 'Going round for dinner?'

'Nice people, aren't they?' Louis said.

I didn't answer. We drove a few streets and then I needed navigation.

'Which way, Louis?'

'You don't remember the way back?'

'No, I don't.'

'Next left at the lights.'

'Shall I follow the car behind us then?'

'What are you talking about?'

'Nothing.'

'Are you losing your marbles or something?'

'More than likely, Louis. I wouldn't be surprised.'

'Fourth exit at the next roundabout.'

I took the third exit. I assumed that was what he meant. The fourth one would have taken us right back the way we had come. He sat there eating May's world-famous Rocky Road as we drove along, with his eyes nearly closed, and his beanie hat down over them.

Sometimes you drive, and time seems suspended. You know your general location, but you don't really know where you are. You could be anywhere.

Yet everywhere you go there's some world-famous thing that you never heard of before. There are so many famous such things in the world, which languish in total obscurity. They seem like drowning men, calling for help, reaching out for a hand to save them, saying to indifferent and tardy strangers that if you knew who I really was, and how much I mattered, you wouldn't hesitate – you'd jump straight in.

15

NUMBERS

Louis got out of the ward after a couple of days, and by then I was able to drive the ute, so we cancelled the hospital car service and I drove him in for the radiotherapy treatment every day.

They give you fifteen to twenty minutes' worth, five days a week for six weeks, and then you're done. You rarely get more than that, even when some time has gone by. The body can only stand so much radiation.

If they gave you the amount of radiation in one session that they gave you over the six weeks, you'd be dead two weeks later.

The routine now was that Louis woke at six, then went to the kitchen, wearing the underpants that had long since gone out of style, then he'd take his anti-nausea and put his glaucoma drops into his eyes. An hour later, he'd take the chemo. An hour later, we'd get into the ute, with Louis wearing the clothes that he'd worn for the last week, and off we'd go to the hospital. His breath was terrible, so maybe it was a good job that the window kept sliding down.

It would take us twenty minutes to get there and I don't remember what we talked about. Nothing important, probably, just morning talk, the kinds of things people say to each other when sitting in commuter tail-backs. We could have listened to the radio, had it been working.

The only thing I recollect is Louis trying to recall that week's car park code. If you were going for radiotherapy, there was a special free car park for you. You were privileged.

'It's four numbers,' he'd say.

'Yes, Louis.'

'Do you know it?'

'No. I can never remember it but it's written down on your appointment card.'

'It's the same as yesterday? It's the same all week, right?'

'Yes.'

'Something to do with the time of day?'

'No, Louis, that's your PIN number.'

'Strictly speaking you should just say PIN.'

'You told me.'

'You listened then?'

'Just habit.'

'It's 1954. That's the car park number.'

'I don't know. I don't remember.'

'Aren't you worried that you don't remember?'

'No.'

'Why not?'

'Louis, nobody can remember everything. Why do you beat yourself up about it?'

'Because I'm screwed. I can't read.'

'You can if you take your time.'

'Is it 1954?'

'You need to look on the back of the card.'

'You look.'

'I can't. I'm driving.'

'Where's my card? Where's my appointment card? Where's the card? Stop driving! I've lost my card. I'm so stupid. I've lost my card. What are we going to do, we've lost the card!'

'Louis – it's in your bag. Your blue bag.'

'Where's my bag? I've lost the bag!'

'Under the seat, Louis.'

'I'm so fucking stupid.'

'Louis, you're anything but. You are not stupid. You just need to take your time. But you panic, and that makes things worse. Just tell yourself – it'll come to me.'

'It's here.'

'Good. So what's the car park code?'

'I can't read it.'

'Is that the right card? Louis, what else have you got in there?'

'That's my drugs and my phone.'

'What's the paper?'

'My will.'

'Louis, you carry your will around? What for?'

'Safe-keeping.'

'You call that bag safe? It gets lost ten times a week.'

'I've left you everything.'

'I don't want anything. Leave it to your friends. Leave it to the cats' home.'

'Never had a cat.'

'Why should that stop you? Leave it to cancer research.'

'There's a few bequests.'

'I know. I've got a copy. It was e-mailed to me, remember?'

'And I've left Bella six-tenths of the house and the rest is mine.'

'Why'd you do that? You broke up twenty years ago.'

'We agreed.'

'Your money, Louis. So what's the car park code?'

'What's that say? What's that sticker say on the back of the appointment card?'

'It says 1954.'

'What'd I say it was earlier?'

'You said 1954.'

'Then I got it right!'

'You did.'

'Nah – you're just saying that to make me feel better.'

'Louis, I am not just saying it. For Christ's sake!'

'We're screwed.'

'Louis, we are not screwed. We're going to get through this. You finish the treatment and then you can book your flights and come over to visit us for a few months.'

'Left here then straight over the underpass.'

We'd get to the hospital with time to spare.

'I'll shout you a flat white.'

We'd go to Starbucks at the main entrance and he'd insist on buying me a coffee. He couldn't drink or eat anything until after the radio. Then we'd walk back to the department, wait, he'd go in for the session. I'd go back to Starbucks and buy him a Danish pastry. I couldn't buy it the first time because if I tried to do that he'd tell me he didn't want it.

I'd sit and read the magazines and look at the other patients and their relatives. About half an hour later Louis would reappear and he'd sit down next to me.

'I'm starving. I've had no breakfast.'

'I got you this.'

So he'd eat the Danish while I fetched him some tea. Then we'd drive away and go to the shops, or there would be another appointment. You could be in that hospital all day, mostly waiting. There's an awful lot of waiting when you're ill. There are social workers to see, occupational therapists, consultants, doctors. A lot of the time, we'd just go home, and Louis would crash out for three or four hours, and I'd try to sort out his impenetrable paperwork and fill in his insurance forms, and his claim forms for the government. When he woke I'd get him to go out for lunch.

'We'll go and see the Malaysian girls for lunch. Have a panini.'

'How come we're spending so much money on lunch? I've been out more times to eat since you got here than I have in the last five years. We can stay in and have cheese on toast.'

'Louis, I'm feeling cooped up in here.'

But once out, he was different. He'd sit at the table, watching the traffic go by, and say, without irony, 'This is the life.'

Though it wasn't. It was the opposite.

In the afternoon, he'd crash out again. I'd go to the supermarket. Some of his friends might call round early evening, bringing beer and encouragement.

Don and Marion lived a few doors down the street. One night, entirely seriously – while Louis was asleep in the back and not there to hear her – she said,

'You know why Louis has the tumour in his head?'

'No, Marion. But I've looked on the internet and it says no one knows the cause. There are theories, but no solid causes.'

'Well, I know.'

'So what was it?'

'Thinking. Louis – always thinking. Every time I see him – thinking. Never stops. Always thinking.'

'But, Marion, isn't everyone constantly thinking all the time? But we don't all get tumours.'

'Not like Louis. Louis, I believe, always thought very deep.'

'Deep thinking gave him a brain tumour?'

'I believe so. He overdid it.'

'Well – I don't know. I mean, say you got stomach cancer instead, what would cause that?'

'Eating the wrong things.'

'So Louis thought the wrong things?'

'It's possible.'

I didn't want to argue it, so we moved on to something else.

I can't go with the being responsible for your own disease theory either. All right, you can unarguably eat, smoke, drink or indiscriminately fornicate yourself to death. But every disease? Leukaemia? Motor neurone disease? Typhoid? The endless list of bad things that happen to people? You're responsible for the mosquito that bites you? For the infection that gets you? For the multiplying cells creating havoc in your body?

Nor am I deeply impressed by the intervention of prayer and the laying on of hands and the phoney 'healing' that seems to cure only those ailments which would cure themselves anyway, given time. If prayer cures people, why does everyone die?

I was watching the news and some twenty people or more had been killed in a multiple car crash. But a woman who had been due to travel along that route that day had had her journey delayed.

'I think God must have been watching over us,' she said.

It seems like a highly selective and random business – who gets forgotten and who gets saved.

16

FREE LUNCH

To get on the internet, it was necessary to tie a dongle to the end of a bamboo pole and stick it out of the window, for otherwise the reception was none too good. Louis showed me how to do it.

'Louis, why don't you just get cable broadband?'

'It's pricey.'

'Louis, it isn't, not really. And think of the convenience. You wouldn't have to tie a dongle to a bamboo pole and then wave it around outside the window looking for a hotspot.'

'It's no good anyway – we're screwed.'

'Louis, it's a small problem easily fixed.'

'I'm going to lie down.'

So he went to bed. Getting cured is an exhausting business. And hospitals are no places for sick and vulnerable people. And everybody knows that, but no one has devised an alternative.

After some heavy persuading, I got Louis and his debit card to go to the electrical warehouse.

'I still don't see why I need a new washing machine.'

'Louis, it doesn't work. It's twenty-five years old and it sticks on each cycle. It doesn't wash clothes, it massacres them. You put pullovers in there and they come out as balls of wool.'

'And the fridge isn't that bad.'

'It's got diseases in it. And it's rusting through.'

'It's lasted this long.'

'Well, it's come to the end of its useful existence.'

That was a mistake, saying that.

'Anyway,' I hurriedly added. 'Let's go and look at them.'

Louis chose a fridge/freezer as near as possible in shape and form to the one he had already.

'I want a top-loader washing machine, like the old one.'

The salesman did a deal as Louis was buying two items and threw in free delivery and the removal of the old fridge and old washing machine.

I noticed there was an offer with the washer.

'Louis – you see this? You get a year's supply of washing powder, free, when you buy this one.'

'How much is a year's supply?'

'Says twelve kilos.'

He looked at me a while, as if doing slow but accurate mental calculations.

'That's more like twenty years.'

'Well, if you can eke it out that long, so much the better.'

So Louis managed to recollect his PIN and he tapped

it in and delivery was promised for Saturday, and so we left.

The machines arrived as promised, but no washing powder.

I called the store and queried this.

'No, you need to apply online,' the salesman said. 'Go on the manufacturer's website and there's a form there. Just put in the serial number and date of purchase and they'll send it on to you.'

I got the dongle and tied it to the bamboo pole.

'What are you doing?'

'Fishing for the internet, Louis. What do you think?'

'No washing powder then?' he said, with a kind of complacency and a grim-edged satisfaction – the satisfaction of one who has prophesied the worst and has seen it come to pass.

'I'm just going to fill the form in online and it'll be on its way.'

'You know your trouble – you're too gullible,' Louis said. 'Credulous and gullible.'

'Louis, it's a bona fide offer.'

'There's no such thing as a free lunch.'

'It's not a free lunch, Louis, it's free washing powder. A year's worth.'

'We'll never see it.'

'Louis – why don't you go and have a lie down?'

'We'll never see it. Not in my lifetime.'

The website said it might take up to six weeks to come. I stayed with Louis for four weeks, and then I had to go home for a time, and then I came back again.

Still no washing powder.

'Louis – are you sure it never came while I was away?'

'Not unless they left it outside and someone stole it.'

'Is that likely?'

'Not the neighbours, but some passer-by.'

'Wouldn't it be a lot to carry?'

'Some people would steal the hairs up your nose.'

'For what purpose, Louis?'

'I'm just saying.'

The washing powder still didn't come. Louis got worse. They took him back into the ward and from there he went to the palliative care, which was a hospice by another name.

'My washing powder come?'

'Not yet, Louis, but I'll e-mail them.'

'I said we'd never get it.'

One day Louis was still walking and he was getting visitors and squeezing their hands with bone-breaking handshakes, just to illustrate how strong he still was.

'Be back up and on your feet in no time,' the visitors would tell him.

A couple of days after that he couldn't get out of bed any more, and then he stopped speaking and all he would do was squeeze your hand softly, and then he stopped even that.

I went back to the house in the morning, for a break from it all and a change of scenery and to see if anything needed doing. I found a card on the mat saying the postman had been, with an item that required a signature and which was too large to go through the letterbox, but it could be picked up from the depot.

I drove to the depot with ID and the collection card

and there was a big box waiting. It was a year's supply of washing powder.

That afternoon I went back to sit with Louis. His hands were cold and his breathing was slow and sighing. A new nurse came in for the afternoon shift.

'How are we doing?'

'His hands seem cold, and kind of clammy.'

'Ah . . .'

She knew more than I did, but even I wasn't that stupid.

At six I went down the road and ate some dinner. I came back and his breathing was even more shallow.

At about nine, I dozed off. I heard the nurses coming in to turn him, but I fell asleep again.

I awoke to silence and darkness. It was half eleven. I soon realised what the silence was, and why it seemed unusual.

'Louis?' I said. 'Louis?'

I went to the bed and touched his arm, then held my hand near his mouth, but felt no breath. I rang the buzzer for the nurse to come. As I sat there waiting for her, I remembered that I hadn't told Louis about his washing powder.

'Louis,' I'd meant to say. 'You may not believe it, but your washing powder turned up. Twelve one-kilo boxes. I put them in the basement. All ready to go.'

But, as is ever the way with prepared and imagined speeches, it didn't go as it should have done, according to purpose and to plan. And the moment was missed, and the timing was all out. There aren't any retakes though, in life – no chances to replay the scene a little better, in a different and a more satisfactory way. There's only the one shot, the one take, and that's it.

So Louis died not knowing his washing powder had turned up. And what, people might cogently argue, did it matter, and what difference did it make, and why was that important in any way at all?

To which questions there are only further questions to act as answers. Namely, what does matter? What does make a difference? What is important? And who is to make the judgement and the call?

I waited until after midnight, then I cycled back to Louis' house on his bike. The highways were empty, there was hardly a car, and the chill night was splendid and clear, with all the stars of the southern hemisphere there visible above.

I got back to Louis' place and tied the dongle to the pole and hung it out of the window and went online. And in this manner, and by this means, I informed those who knew him, had cared for him, had been acquainted with him, and who had loved him, that he was no more.

The twelve packets of washing powder were still down there in the morning. I opened the box and took out the packets, and gave them away to the neighbours and to Louis' friends.

I took to riding his bike around the neighbourhood, while wearing disreputable shorts and T-shirts with spatters of paint upon them, and I didn't trouble to shave. I travelled his tracks and went to his haunts, and there must have been those who had not heard of his illness, for I swear that as I cycled along a wide-brimmed street and passed a gang of workmen fixing a roof, I heard a voice call,

'Hey, how are you, Louis? How are you doing?'

But I had no time to stop, so I just raised my hand in greeting and sped on. I cycled through the park and along by the trees where the fruit bats hung, still smelling fruity and slightly off. I rode past the pitches with the posts and the teams playing Australian Rules football. I rode out past Kangaroo Point, where the personal trainers shepherded their flocks and taught them the moves and the recipes for the dish of fitness, youth and looks.

I rode on by the river and past the Spiegel Tent, which looked tawdry in the daylight, with its sparkling mirrors seeming chipped and only half reflecting. Then I headed for Stones Corner and the Chinese girls, and I went in and got a haircut. And I said,

'Do you remember my coming in with my brother? Lots of hair and eyebrows and plenty of beard?'

But they didn't recall.

And then, with trimmed eyebrows and fashionable haircut, I walked a short way down the street and sat at our usual table and I ordered a flat white and a panini from the Malaysian waitress.

When she brought it over, I said, 'I feel kind of cold today. I wonder if you could light the burner?'

And she looked at me as if I was crazy, because it was getting on for thirty degrees.

'I'm on my own today,' I said. 'My brother's not with me. We'd usually both be here, as you might recall. But he couldn't make it today.'

So she lit the burner for me, and I sat there perspiring. I left a decent tip for her, and then cycled on. She turned the burner off, soon as I went. After that, I didn't look back.

I stopped off at the supermarket to get some food, but I didn't buy any strawberries, as they looked kind of pricey.

Then I went back to the house and I sat at the kitchen table, and I made some tea. And that was what I did. It was the only tune I knew how to play.

Into the world we tumble, and we have no choice. We love whom we find – parents, siblings. We must love them somehow or other, and there is nothing we can do. They might not be right for us, or suit our tastes, or be incompatible, or entirely wrong. We might end up hating and resenting them somewhere down the line. But never entirely, rarely without a glimpse of possible forgiveness and reunion. We love whom we must, and then we grow, and love whom we will. But still we're caught, like a fish with a swallowed hook, and we can swim downriver nearly all our lives, but end up getting tugged back to the past, to childhood, to our defenceless selves, and we are reeled in.

17

ASHES

'I need to get rid of the boat. It's probably worth twenty thousand,' Louis said. He was sitting there, looking agitated, with a demand for money in front of him.

'Yeah, maybe. That only trouble is it'll cost forty to do up.'

'Still a bargain,' Louis said.

'Why do you need to get rid of it?'

'The mooring fees are due. Five thousand.'

'You've got the money. Why not pay it and keep the boat?'

'I can't keep it – the boat. I can't drive to the harbour any more. If I'm not fit to drive a car, how can I sail a boat? I can't even manage the bits and pieces.'

'What do you want me to do, Louis?'

'Find a buyer.'

Easier said.

Louis had built a boat himself, then traded it in for a twenty-six foot ketch, and he and Kirstin – when she had come along – had sailed it up the east coast and to the Barrier Reef, taking a long and easy six months to do so, there and back.

The photographs showed sunny days and the two of them smiling, and the magnets on the rusty fridge saying: *Depression – you are not alone* were forgotten. But then they came back, and the old black dog must have been waiting in the kennels, for a few months later Louis was brooding again over past losses and present dissatisfactions, and it was back to the bum jobs and no strawberries. And then he and Kirstin broke up. And I knew why, but wasn't supposed to tell anyone.

We tried to sell the boat but could find no serious buyers. So Louis decided it was best to cut his losses and to give it away to a good home.

I put an ad in Gumtree – Free twenty-six foot ketch. Needs some work but otherwise sound. Collect.

It is a widely held opinion that too many people in this world want something for nothing. But when you actually try to do that – to give something away, for absolutely nothing – you find that the contention is not based on the facts. People are suspicious of something for nothing. They approach it warily, and kind of sniff at it, and give it a poke, ready to run off as if it might lunge at them.

Or they are choosy. More choosy than if they were actually paying. Were they paying, they might think, 'Yeah, it's not a hundred per cent, but it's a bargain. Needs some doing up, but so what? I'll take a chance.'

But when it's free, they want to know what the catch is, and what they're letting themselves in for, and they don't trust you much at all.

There were time-wasters and fender-kickers and guys who tapped the mast and said, Hmmm – they'd need to think about it, or check with their wives, or, on second thoughts, they didn't know how to sail a boat anyway and it might be too late in life to learn.

Or they wanted to live on it, or grow marijuana plants in it, or go round the world in it, or escape their troubles in it, or more likely they just wanted something to do to kill a Sunday afternoon. Or they lived two hundred miles away, though they promised to be there on Thursday, and come the Saturday after, you still hadn't heard from them.

Eventually a woman and a man who lived a few miles away said they'd take it, and they came round and we exchanged documents and Louis gave them the keys.

'When we've fixed it up, Louis,' the man taking it said, 'you've got a standing invitation to come out in it. Any time. Just call. Whenever you like. Many times as you like.'

But Louis just looked sad-eyed under his beanie and shook his head and said,

'It's your boat now. You do what you want with it, Cliff. It's yours.'

They took the keys and left.

'One less thing to worry about then, Louis,' I said. 'You don't have to pay the mooring fees now.'

'I loved that boat,' he said. 'Going down to the marina, chewing the fat.'

'When did you last go anywhere in it?'

'Up the coast with Kirstin.'

'That was ten years ago, Louis.'

'A couple of times round the bay since, maybe. I'd be down there every weekend though, doing the bits and pieces.'

'Which bits and pieces, Louis?'

'The boating ones. Go down, see Hugh—'

'Who's Hugh?'

'Moored next to me. You met him. Irish Hugh.'

'I thought he sounded Welsh.'

'He is.'

'So why's he called Irish?'

'You wouldn't understand,' Louis said. 'They're just like that down there. You'd need to have a boat.'

After the funeral the ashes were delivered to the door. I had to sign for them and show ID. The man who delivered them was still in his dark undertaker's suit and wore a white starched shirt and sober tie.

He left me and Louis together, so I rang Irish Hugh up and said,

'Hugh?'

'Louis? Is that you, you cunt?'

'No, Hugh. It's his brother. I'm just using his phone. You were at the service, Hugh. You came to the crematorium. You stood up and said a few words. How could Louis be ringing you up?'

'I forgot. It was his name coming up on my phone.'

'I've got his ashes here, Hugh.'

'Your brother, he was a right cunt. I told him I'd take that boat off his hands and do it up and look after it for him until he got better and then he could have had it back.'

'He didn't get better, Hugh.'

'Didn't know that at the time. And what does he do – he gives it away to bloody strangers. They were down here yesterday, sailing round in Louis' boat like they owned it.'

'They do, Hugh.'

'They looked like cunts to me.'

'Hugh—'

'How are you keeping anyway? You clearing out the house?'

'Trying to. You know his will's gone missing?'

'Surprised he made one.'

'He did and he carried it around in a blue cooler bag with all his bits and pieces.'

'His bits and whats?'

'Pieces. The drugs he had to take and his appointment cards. But it's all gone missing.'

'No will? None at all?'

'There's a copy.'

'You're laughing then.'

'Not really. A copy's not legal enough. It might be challenged. The court might say that Louis had destroyed the original – so the copy's no longer valid.'

'I think you might need a solicitor, boyo.'

'I've got one. That's not why I'm calling.'

'It's bloody windy down here. Even the seagulls look seasick. Can you hear all that rigging rattling? It's like the steelworks at Port Talbot. Or have they closed them down?'

'Hugh, can you take us all out in your cruiser to scatter the ashes, say next weekend?'

'Who's invited?'

'You and Mrs Hugh and your son Hugh, obviously, and

maybe his kids, and, say, Louis' friend Halley, and the neighbours, Don and Marion, and Kirstin and me.'

'I can probably fit them on, but that's your limit.'

'The weather going to be good?'

'Sunday? All right in the morning. Get here before it blows up.'

'When?'

'Ten'll do.'

'Thanks, Hugh.'

'I'd have looked after that boat for him and given it back to him though. I liked your brother Louis, I had a lot of time for him, but he was a cunt.'

'He was fearsomely independent, Hugh, and didn't like being beholden to people.'

'That's just what I'm saying if you'd listen to me – he was a cunt.'

'But you're okay about the ashes?'

'I'd have been offended if you hadn't asked me.'

'Thanks, Hugh.'

'Here – my wife was saying that you're quite a bit like your brother.'

'You mean I'm a cunt as well, do you, Hugh?'

'I'll see you Sunday then, shall I?'

'Thanks, Hugh.'

'You'll bring the ashes with you, will you?'

'No, I'll leave them here.'

'Well, there won't be much point in—'

'Joking, Hugh.'

'Your brother had a peculiar sense of humour as well. But I'd have looked after that boat for him and given it back to him when he got better.'

'He died, Hugh.'

'I know. And I told him he should have gone to the doctor a year ago. He'd sit on that boat of his and stare out to sea for hours on end. Just sit there, staring, until I'd go over and tell him to put the kettle on and we'd have a cup of tea.'

'I'll see you Sunday, then, Hugh.'

'I'll see you Sunday, Louis. And don't forget your ashes.'

'It's not Louis, Hugh, it's his—'

But the phone had gone dead.

I guess there's good and bad in everyone; the trouble is it's usually so stirred in with the blender that you can't separate the one from the other.

Hugh told me once that he was seventy-six years old, though he looked no more than sixty, but he did dye his hair. He told me he never drank and then poured us both a whisky and he lit a cigarette to go with it. He had done every job there is to do under the sun, apart, maybe, from be a midwife, and even then he might have seen some action at an amateur level.

On the following Sunday, Halley and Kirstin and Marion and Don and I drove down to the marina in two cars and found Irish Hugh, Mrs Hugh, their son, Hugh, and Hugh's son – surprisingly not called Hugh – waiting on the boat.

We set sail and headed out to the bay. After an hour, younger Hugh, who was steering, cut the engine and threw the anchor out.

'How's this?'

'Perfect,' I said.

The sky was blue, the sun high, the breeze cooling, the clouds few.

I had trouble getting the lid off the canister and had to ask Hugh for a screwdriver so I could prise it up. Then Marion uncorked the bottle of Jägermeister she had brought, and Mrs Hugh passed round the teacups, and we drank a toast to absent friends.

Then I tipped the ashes over to leeward so that they wouldn't blow back into our faces, and Louis sped away, returning to the elements, becoming part of the vast ocean. It would carry him all around the world. In a year or two there would be a trace of Louis in all the seas and oceans of the planet.

The Jägermeister bottle was empty, so Hugh broke out the Greek brandy from the First Aid cabinet, so we drank that too, and then Marion passed out on one of the bunks for half an hour. When the brandy was gone, younger Hugh produced an eskie – a cool box – with beer in it.

'Louis would have liked it here,' I said to Hugh, the elder.

'Sailed out here many a time,' he said.

'What's the island there?' I asked. 'The one nearest to us?'

'Old prison island,' Hugh said. 'They used to keep convicts there.'

'Convicts?'

'That's right. They sent the convicts to Australia, and when they got here, the ones that were so crooked even the convicts couldn't stand them, they sent them to that island there. Could never swim it to the mainland. The sharks'd get you first.'

'I see. So we have just scattered Louis' ashes offshore from a prison island, once occupied by Australia's worst convicts?'

'He loved it out here, Louis did.'

'Can I have another beer, Hugh?'

'Help yourself, boyo. Let's have a toast – to Louis.'

'To Louis.'

'I loved him. But he was a cunt.'

'Hugh!' his wife rebuked him.

'Sorry, love. No offence.'

Mrs Hugh had brought flowers, which I had overlooked to bring, and she handed us a few each, and we dropped them into the sea, to follow the ashes on their way.

Soon there was a pageant of drifting blossoms, mixing with the deep blue of the water and the flick of the white-caps' foam.

'Better get back, Dad,' Hugh the younger said. 'Blowing up now a bit, and look at the horizon.'

He hauled in the anchor and we turned back for the marina. Shoals of jellyfish floated alongside, white as the flowers we had thrown.

We tied up at the marina and headed for lunch at Fried Fish.

'Nice to see you again,' the waiter said when we arrived.

'I'll have the usual,' I told him, when he returned to take the order.

'Your brother not here today?' he asked.

The next day Hugh rang me early.

'Louis? That you?'

'No, Hugh, it's his—'

'Ah, you're the one I want. Not too early for you, is it?'

'Well, it is only half seven.'

'I'm down here by five every morning.'

'Doing what?'

'Sorting things out.'

'Hugh, what things need sorting out at five in the—?'

'Thing is, I've been sweeping bits of your brother off the deck.'

'Sorry. I tried to make sure that didn't happen.'

'I think there's some of him in the compass.'

'I don't think – I mean, how would he get in there?'

'But it don't matter, boyo. No, the reason I'm calling is you left the canister behind.'

'Yes, I realised. Sorry. I was going to call later when you were up.'

'I am up. Up every morning at four thirty, down here on the marina and on my boat for five. Don't really know why. There's sod all to do. So I thought I'd give you a ring. You want the canister back?'

'Not particularly. It's only plastic.'

'No sentimental value then?'

'Not really.'

'No, it's not like it was a coat or his trousers or something, is it? Tell you what, I'll put it in the recycling then.'

'Thanks.'

'That was a nice coffin you got him, by the way.'

'It was wicker.'

'He'd have liked that. He always liked alternatives. I'm thinking of having one of those myself. I said to Mary, I'll have a woven one.'

'Well, good to talk to you, Hugh, and thanks again.'

'When are you going back?'

'Still got a bit to sort out. Another two weeks or so.'

'Come down and have a cup of tea then.'

139

'Thanks, Hugh.'

'See you then, Louis.'

'I'm not—'

And he hung up.

I felt as if I'd spent a lifetime in the shadows of tall trees, walking down a track of old footsteps – as if dinosaurs had once passed that way, and you could still hear the echoes of their rumbling. And every time you tried to get a bit of attention for yourself, someone would remember them.

18

SEE RED

I wasn't supposed to know about the Kirstin episode, at least not as far as other people were concerned, for I was sworn to confidence, but know about it I did.

I never met her until the funeral. Louis had left her a bequest in his will – or at least in the copy of it I possessed – and so plainly still carried some small burning candle for her which the slipstream of the years flying by had failed to extinguish.

I had no number for her, but found one for her daughter on one of the pieces of paper with coffee-cup rings on them that acted as Louis' address book. I rang and introduced myself and said could you please tell your mother that Louis from ten years back has died of a tumour and this is his brother and he has left her something and she would be very welcome to attend the funeral service, but if not, no problem, and everyone would understand. But, in either event, would she have an address for her mother as the lawyer would want to be in touch.

Ten minutes later Kirstin rang back and sounded genuinely sorry that Louis had gone. She seemed perplexed that he had left her anything and said she felt she could not accept it. This was in strong contrast to some beneficiaries of wills, who often feel they should have been left a whole lot more.

'Kirstin,' I said, 'the wording in the will says: To my friend Kirstin, three thousand dollars. To my friend, is the phrase he used. My friend. I think he wanted you to have it. Don't you?'

She turned up at the funeral, both she and her daughter. Two nicer people you would not meet.

'Louis,' I thought. 'What went wrong?'

But I knew what had gone wrong.

Louis had tried to strangle her.

Inexcusable, but excuse it I must, even though I feel like the body-in-the-bath murderer saying, It was just the one lousy corpse.

It was after the halcyon sailing trip up the coast, and they had been back a while, and the old black dog was nibbling at Louis' heels.

He always had the yearning in him to strike out on his own and to be his own boss, but every time he tried it, things seemed not to work out, and it was back to the drudgery of some ill-paid assembly line.

The two of them set up in a franchise business, but it went wrong. They spent a lot of money up front, but little was coming in. Kirstin wanted to stick at it, but Louis wanted to cut their losses and quit.

Then, one morning, Louis rang me.

'Louis, you don't sound good. You ill?'

'No, but I've done something terrible.'

'Well?'

'It was Kirstin. We were in the kitchen and having an argument, and suddenly I saw red, and the next thing I know – when I came to – I had my hands round her neck.'

I didn't know what to say.

'Well – that's bad, Louis, but it's not as if you do it all the time.'

'No.'

'I mean, that's a first, isn't it?'

'Yes, yes.'

'We all have bad days, Louis.'

'Yeah, but I tried to strangle her. And didn't even know I was doing it.'

'Yeah. I can see where you're coming from, Louis, and it isn't good. But, I mean, you stopped – you did stop, didn't you? Louis, she isn't dead, is she?'

'No, no. No, no, no. But she's gone.'

'Right.'

'And she's not coming back, she says.'

'Yeah—'

'I feel so bad—'

'Oh, Louis – why do you live so far away?'

'I feel – I mean – I've never done anything, ever. I just saw red. I just saw red.'

'I know, Louis. I understand.'

'I could have killed her.'

'You didn't.'

'But I could have done.'

'Louis, why don't you grab a plane and come on over and see us and we can go around and visit the old places?'

'It would be nice, but I can't right now. I've got to find a job and—'

'Louis, are you all right?'

'Not really.'

'Come over, Louis.'

'Have you ever strangled anyone?'

'I've thought about it.'

'Who have you thought of strangling?'

'You.'

'Yeah, funny.'

'Oh, you think I'm joking?'

'She's gone and I don't think she's ever coming back.'

'Come over, Louis, why don't you just come on over?'

'I can't. I've got to get a job.'

'Louis, what's life for?'

'Maybe next year.'

'You always—'

'I feel so bad about it.'

'Try calling her.'

'She won't answer.'

'Louis, are you all right?'

'No, not really, I'm not.'

'Louis, you're my brother. I don't care what you've done. I mean, I'm not endorsing it, but—'

'I just saw red. I didn't know what I was doing. I just saw red.'

'You're a good person, Louis. Really. Remember that stuffed koala bear you sent? Dan loves it.'

'He does?'

'He winds it up and it plays "Waltzing Matilda". And Kelly, she loves the kangaroo.'

'How's the boomerang?'

'Still coming back.'

'You got it to work then?'

'Sort of. Are you all right, Louis?'

'I'll maybe call you tomorrow.'

'If you don't, I'll call you. Come over and see us, Louis.'

'I can't. I can't right now.'

'Louis—'

'I've got to go now.'

'I'm going to call you tomorrow.'

'Did they really like the toys?'

'Do you want me to go and get them and put them on the phone?'

'No, it's all right. Say Louis says Hi. Don't tell them about the strangling.'

'Louis, they're kids. I'm not going to tell anyone.'

'Thanks. Okay. I couldn't help it, didn't know what I was doing.'

'We're all still alive, Louis. Nobody died. Nobody got killed.'

'Maybe talk to you tomorrow.'

'If you don't ring me I'll ring you.'

'Okay then.'

'Bye.'

*

Of such mistakes is life compounded. Louis, for years the gentlest and most considerate of men, snapped, and saw red, and he lost her and frightened her. And she would never risk going back, although she loved him and he loved her. And that was it. No going back. And the next time they were in the same room, he lay in a wickerwork casket, and she sat in a pew. So of such errors and mistakes and sadnesses is life constructed, and who, if they had some kind of repair kit upon them, would not rush to the latest emergency or scene of crime, and apply the healing powers and the make-and-do and the make-and-mend and the stitch-in-time and make things better and put things right?

Who would not do that if they could? Who would not wipe clean the slate and reset the clocks and let the runners run again after their unintentional false start? But nobody can. The bad things are done, and may even be forgiven up to a point, but they can't be written out; nobody can pretend they did not happen. And you can never, never, never go back.

When we went out on the boat that day to scatter Louis' ashes, Kirstin told me how much she had missed him, and had thought of going back to him, but never had. She didn't know that I knew what had happened, she just referred to an incident and talked in general terms.

There was no one else for either of them. The older you get, maybe the harder it is to find that compatible soul. And the years that could have been spent otherwise go by in isolation and even loneliness. And that's how it is for people. That's how it often is. And you can sit on the train and read your magazine or go home and watch the TV show, but it doesn't make one iota of difference. Because that's just the paint and decorations. And that's just how it is. That's how we are. That's how it is for us. That's how we live.

19

PHASCOGALE

Louis said you had to keep the lids on the jars and the fridge door shut tight, because there was a creature that came into the house called a phascogale. He said it was carnivorous, but that wouldn't stop it climbing in with the vegetables or gnawing on the cornflakes to see if it liked them.

'A what-go-gale?'

'Phascogale.'

'Fast?'

'Why don't you look it up in the bits and pieces?' he said.

So I did, and got a picture of it. It was small – a small marsupial, quite nice and amiable-looking in its way, with rather large eyes. It was about the size of a squirrel. I saw it once or twice, hiding under the eaves, but mostly it kept its distance and didn't bother us much.

I started to get interested in its private life, and read up a little more about it.

'Louis,' I said, 'did you know that the male phascogale dies after it has sex?'

'No,' Louis said. 'I didn't know that. You think I'm some kind of pervert voyeur who stalks small creatures?'

'Don't you think that's interesting, though, Louis?'

'It's interesting for the phascogale,' he said. 'But then, being a phascogale, it doesn't know what it's got coming to it. Whereas, if it were human . . .'

And he was right of course. We know what we've got coming to us. That's what distinguishes us from the other and so-called lesser creatures. It isn't that we walk upright or have developed languages of extensive vocabulary capable of expressing fine shades of meaning. Nor is it that we have prehensile fingers and thumbs.

No, the main thing is that we know what we've got coming. And maybe, if we didn't know that, we too might be happily chewing the grass in the fields, or plucking the plums off the branches, or drinking water from a pool – not worrying about the cholera, typhoid, parasites and worms that might be in there. That's the trouble – we don't know enough and we don't know all we need to know, but we still know too much.

'Don't you think that's weird, Louis, that the male has sex with the female and then dies?'

'You mean she kills him? It wouldn't surprise me. Like a black widow spider. They mate, and she does for him. Or ants. They mate, and same thing, they're left to die.'

'But getting back to the phascogale, Louis, where is the evolutionary advantage in the male phascogale not being around?'

'He doesn't have to listen to the nagging?' Louis said.

'What about his genes?'

'Well, he's reproduced, hasn't he?' Louis said. 'His genes are safe. He no longer has a function or purpose. So he dies.'

'But isn't that true of a lot of mammals?'

'He's not a mammal. He's a marsupial.'

'So are kangaroos. But the males don't die after they've mated.'

'Maybe he hops off before she can get him.'

'But the female doesn't kill the male, that's what I'm saying. He just dies.'

'Then at least he goes out on a high.'

'Would you have sex the once if you knew it was going to kill you?'

'There are worse ways of committing suicide,' Louis said.

'I really do not see the Darwin in it,' I said. 'I do not see the evolutionary logic behind it at all. If he lived, he could help provide.'

'Maybe he's a lazy bastard,' Louis said. 'Maybe all these male phascogales are lazy bastards who'd live on benefits if you let them.'

'You know what it means, though, Louis? It means that every phascogale family is a single-parent family. The phas-cogales are brought up by the mothers and the father is not around.'

'Having died of fornicating?'

'Exactly. You look at Mum, Louis. Now she was left a single parent and brought us both up, right?'

'She wasn't a phascogale, though.'

'Louis, I know that. You think I don't know that our own mother was a woman and not a phascogale?'

'Why do you take everything so seriously?'

'I thought that was you who did that.'

'What's your point?'

'They're all single-parent families, Louis. That's my point. None of the little phascogales ever has a father. No growing phascogale ever knows its dad. Do you know the correlation, Louis, between being brought up in a family without a father and juvenile delinquency and the incidence of depression?'

'So what are you saying now? You're saying that phascogales are juvenile delinquents, suffering with bipolar disorder?'

'For Chrissake, Louis.'

'What?'

'I'm just saying where is the evolutionary advantage in forcing children to grow up psychologically damaged?'

'You think phascogales are psychologically damaged? You think that's why they've been coming into the kitchen and getting the tops off my jars?'

'No, not necessarily. But possibly – if animals can feel emotions the way we do – they might look around and not see their fathers and feel kind of sad.'

'No. Definitely not, no.'

'Why?'

'Because you only feel deprived by comparison. If you look around and see all the other phascogales don't have fathers either, then you won't feel deprived.'

'You might notice that other animals have fathers.'

'No. They wouldn't. They'd only be interested in their own species. You're just being anthropomorphic.'

'So are you.'

'No. I'm being logical.'

'Yeah, you're Mr Spock, Louis.'

'What?'

'Louis – don't you think not having a father is damaging?'

'It's all too late now. What difference does it make? We can't bring him back. And if he'd lived, he'd be an old, old, man now, if he was still here. And we'd be saying what a pain he was that he'd lost his marbles. Or maybe we'd have fallen out. You got away with murder when you were a teenager. If you'd had a father there you wouldn't have had it so easy.'

'Easy? Louis, look at yourself. These jobs you do, all this working with your hands – when you're capable of—'

'That's what I missed, that he wasn't there to show us how to do things, how to use tools, how to—'

'Louis, he didn't want you to work using tools. He wanted you to get educated.'

'Those people that you have to work with in those white-collar places, these labs, these universities, they've got no authenticity. It's all ass-licking and politics.'

'Louis, do you seriously believe that? You think there's no ass-licking and politics on the factory floor? You really think that sawing wood and bending steel and unblocking drains is some kind of noble calling that, say, being a chemist isn't? We wouldn't have anything if it wasn't for people using their brains. If using your hands is so noble, why isn't using your head?'

'I thought we were talking about phascogales.'

'Yeah, well – as an illustration.'

'Of what?'

'I just don't see any evolutionary advantage, Louis, in not having a father.'

He looked at me from under the beanie hat.

'Well, we're not going to know now, are we?' he said. 'It's done. We're the same as the phascogale.'

'Our dad died, yeah.'

'No. We're screwed.'

'Don't start that again, Louis. We are going to get through all this.'

'You were there. You heard the consultant. You know the chances.'

'I heard what he had to say. Five, six, seven years, and by that time they may have found—'

'No. Five to ten per cent survive five years. Nearer five. Five per cent. Twenty per cent are alive after two years. The rest – a year to eighteen months. Eighty per cent chance, almost, of not lasting eighteen months.'

'Louis, we have to think positive.'

'No, we have to think practical. I'm tired. I'm going to lie down.'

I left food out that night for the phascogale. But she never came and took it. I threw it in the bin in the morning before Louis would notice it, and then we drove to the hospital for Louis' radiotherapy again. We had time for Starbucks, so he shouted me a flat white. I said I'd get him a Danish. He said he didn't want one. We went to the radiotherapy department. While he was in treatment, I went back to Starbucks and bought him a Danish and returned to the waiting area. When he came out of treatment he said he was starving, so I gave him the Danish and made him a cup of tea at the sink and kettle unit for the use of patients and their relatives.

Louis drank his tea and ate his Danish and I said, 'What shall we do now?'

He said, 'I'll show you the city.'

So we drove down to the river and he showed me around and I thought what a splendid city it was, and I liked the wide streets and the flowing water and the speeding ferries and the feel of the place. I thought that maybe I could have lived there, and had a different life. And who would I have been then?

We caught a tourist boat and went on a trip downriver and back. It was cool but sunny and we sat up on the top deck and ordered a couple of flat whites and drank them as we sailed along, and Louis pointed out the sights to me, and said, 'See there, that's where they have the Sunday market, that's where I met Kirstin and used to have my jewellery stall.' And he was smiling under his beanie hat, and the milky eyes were sparkling.

'What did she sell?'

'She was an artist.'

We returned to the embarkation point and strolled on along the walkway, until we came to a café there.

'Shall we get some lunch, Louis?'

'Looks pricey,' he said.

But what the hell, we had some anyway, and we sat and lingered over the meal and the drinks and we talked of yesterday, and before we knew it, it was late afternoon.

'I'm whacked,' he said. 'You want to go?'

We walked back to the ute and drove home. Louis went straight to his room and crashed out cold.

It was, in its way, a perfect day, like in the Lou Reed song. All the small unexpected things that line up just as you want them, and there isn't a blemish on the cloth.

'That was a good day, wasn't it, Louis?' I called to him, as he headed for his bed.

'It was all right,' he said. A short while later I heard him snoring.

He didn't wake up until five the next morning, when he took his anti-nausea and then his chemo an hour later.

We drove to the hospital.

We got there early, so we went to Starbucks and he insisted on shouting me a flat white.

'Your money's no good here,' he said.

'Louis,' I said. 'Let me get you a Danish for later.'

'I don't want one,' he said. 'I'm not hungry.'

You know how the rest of it goes.

You know how it goes on from there.

That's how it was, every radiotherapy morning, back when Louis was still alive.

I did feel sorry for those phascogales for a while. But then I realised I was being ridiculous. It wasn't the phascogales who were worrying. They were just getting on with looking for food, and mating, and then dying afterwards. Maybe they were happy with that. Maybe they didn't expect anything else – or, more likely, anything at all.

It's in the matter of expectations – that's where we go so wrong.

20

OBSERVER

You get worried sometimes that people might go wandering – go wandering and not come back, and then somebody might ask you what happened to them, and say, Weren't you responsible? And, Weren't you looking out for them?, which you can't be, not all the time.

The operation is called 'debulking'. It is not removal. It is a matter of reducing the mass. A tumour in the brain cannot be excised because to do so would mean to remove good tissue along with the bad – and the possible consequent loss of many things: vision, hearing, balance, personality, cognition, thought processes, motor skills. The edges of the tumour are not clearly defined. Often they are tentacle- and thread-like. As much of the tumour as can be safely removed is, then the remaining cells are bombarded with radiation and chemistry. Few people have part of the brain removed and remain just as they were. There is usually something lost.

We were in the supermarket, and I looked up from the frozen foods to discover that Louis was no longer beside me. I took the trolley and went looking for him. I found him by the yoghurts.

'Louis—'

'Yeah?'

'You all right?'

'I'm all right.'

'I thought you were with me, Louis.'

'In what sense?'

'I thought you were right behind me.'

'Ah.'

'I thought we were getting the groceries.'

'We are.'

'What are you doing, Louis? Why are you just standing here?'

The beanie hat was pulled down low. The beard was getting wild again. There was paint and oil on Louis' old shirt, and some holes in it too. He was wearing his working shorts – but then, all his shorts were working shorts, even the ones he slept in. Or maybe they were his sleeping shorts and I just couldn't tell the difference.

At the end of the aisle a security man was keeping an eye on us. Maybe he was bored and hoping for excitement. Even so, why look for the obvious? Why wouldn't the shoplifter be smartly and soberly dressed, so as to attract little attention? Wouldn't that make more sense?

'Louis – Louis – are you coming? You want to get a pizza tonight? Louis, what are you doing?'

'I'm looking.'

'What are you looking at?'

'Everyone.'

'What are you looking for?'

'I'm trying to see who's got a brain tumour.'

'Louis, how are you going to know that?'

'I'll know.'

'Louis, a tumour is on the inside, not the outside. How are you going to tell?'

'I'll know. I do it all the time. I look at people and I think, Have you got a brain tumour too?'

'So . . .'

He showed no signs of moving, so I stood with him and watched the trolley pushers go by. The security man was slowly but surely coming up the aisle towards us.

'Have you seen any yet?'

'Not yet. I had a possible earlier.'

'Where?'

'But he's gone. I decided it wasn't a tumour. It was just learning difficulties.'

'Well, that's a relief.'

'You see that woman there, and the man with her?'

'They look all right to me.'

'I think he's got a tumour in its early stages but it hasn't been diagnosed yet. You see the way he's acting? That's a tumour way of behaving.'

I watched the man, but he looked all right to me; he behaved no differently to anyone else.

'What's the tumour way? He seems fine.'

'He looks a little confused, and slow. You see the way he's staring at the prices. He's trying to make sense of them and he can't. He's having trouble processing the information and he doesn't know why. He doesn't want to worry the woman and he doesn't want to worry himself. But he is worried and he knows something's wrong. And he doesn't want to go to the doctor and get the bad news. But he'll have to.'

'Louis, I don't think you can tell that from—'

'It's an affinity. Like with gays.'

'What about them?'

'They can spot each other. Gaydar.'

'And you've got tumour-dar?'

'You don't believe me, you go and ask him.'

'Sure, Louis, I'm going to ask a total stranger in a supermarket if he thinks he might have a brain tumour.'

The security guard was almost upon us now.

'How about this guy, Louis? This guy in the uniform? Does he look like he might have a tumour?'

'No. He looks like he might not have a brain at all.'

'Don't cause trouble, Louis.'

'How can I? I'm an invalid.'

The security guard approached with politeness and reserved hostility.

'Everything all right here, gentlemen? There a problem here at all?'

'Yeah,' Louis said. 'The food's pricey.'

'We're okay,' I told the guard. 'We'd just forgotten something. But we're okay now. My brother's just a little unwell.'

'I've got a big bloody brain tumour. Or rather, I haven't,' Louis said. 'It's been taken out. So I've got a big bloody hole instead.'

'Can you point me towards the pizzas?' I said.

159

'Next aisle,' the security man said. Then, 'Is he okay?'

'We're fine,' I told him. 'Louis – you coming?'

We moved on and got the rest of what we needed. Louis had no interest in what we were getting at all. He was keeping his eyes peeled for brain tumours.

'Louis, if you find someone that looks like they definitely have a brain tumour, what are you going to do? Say hi? Swap experiences?'

'Maybe,' he said. 'Birds of a feather and strength in numbers. If you're interested in boats, you hang round with guys with boats. Same thing. Like a club.'

'Louis . . .'

'What?'

'Nothing.'

We waited in the line to pay for the groceries. I noticed that Louis was intently studying a man's head.

'Louis,' I hissed.

'What?'

'If you keep staring you're going to irritate people.'

'Him,' he said. 'Him. Definitely.'

'You can't know that, Louis, not from the back of his head. They had to give you a scan, remember? You can't just tell by looking.'

'I can. Wait until he turns.'

The man turned side on, ready to bag up his purchases.

'There, see.'

He had a large elliptical scar on the side of his head and his hair was shaved.

'You believe me now?'

'He might have been in a fight or something. Or had an accident.'

160

But Louis just gave me one of his smug and satisfied I-knew-I-was-right looks. I found his patronising attitude rather irritating and always had. Funny how people can do that. Even at a time when you ought to be forgiving them anything and putting up without complaint with everything they can throw at you; even when you know that you're going to feel bad that you weren't more tolerant and patient and accommodating; even with all that – they can still get on your nerves.

I look at the people in the supermarket too now, and I wonder if they have what I have – or if I have what they do – and what traits and concerns we might hold in common.

I wonder who's happy and who's lonely and who's sick at heart. I see the men and women with young children and wonder how tired and exasperated they are today. Or I see the expectant woman and wonder how happy she is, and how apprehensive. Or it's the lovers, all wrapped up in each other and themselves – and who can't remember that, if they once experienced it, and who wouldn't give some substantial savings to feel that way again?

I wonder how irritated people are with each other, or content.

But, unlike Louis, I don't think you can tell easily. I think most people go out well-disguised. You don't know the half of how they feel inside. Most of them just look normal and ordinary. Like you. Like me. Maybe.

21

INTERLUDE

To my left was an opera singer, and to my right was an acrobat. The acrobat was a foot juggler, so we have to make the joke. No, she did not take her feet off and juggle with them. What she did was to lie on a small ramp on stage and use her feet to juggle objects and to keep them in the air – things like hoops, balls, small barrels. And she was very adept.

She was small in stature, not slim, but compact. She was in the seat by the window; the opera singer was by the aisle. I was stuck between them. We were eight miles up in the sky and eleven hours' flying time from Singapore.

I hadn't been able to get on to the internet to grab an aisle seat with some extra leg-room for myself, so, the flight being full, I took what I was given, and that was what I got.

In the rows behind us were various other artistes – more acrobats, tumblers, trapeze artists, high-wire specialists, a guy who did a routine involving two ropes and a lot of bath water.

They were headed for Australia, the same as me, going to put on a show at an arts festival there. With the exception of the opera singer, they were German. The singer was American, but she too lived in Berlin. She had married a German, she told me, but it hadn't worked out, and after seven years they had divorced.

I guessed she was in her early thirties, but it was hard to tell. The captain had turned the lights down by now, and the porthole blinds had been closed. People had eaten their tray meals and drunk their wine and were settling down for the night, or watching movies with their headphones plugged into their ears.

As we flew, she told me a little about herself, about the small town without ambition that she had come from in the American heartlands; of her large collection of siblings and their problems and difficulties, and how she was the only one to fly the coop; of how her brothers and sisters were also divorced and separated, though her parents were still together; of how they had financial problems, and she helped out when she could.

But work was had to get. Singing opera was a hard and competitive and often unappreciated business. She had known some lean years and had been thinking of giving up singing and finding something else, when this had come along – singing with this troupe of acrobats in this show. She punctuated the acts with another kind of entertainment. The show was doing well and had been positively received around the globe. But she only had a short-term contract for a limited run, and what then?

All the same, her mind, she told me, was in a good place, and so was she. She was thinking positive, because that was what you had to do. Those who thought positive would be successful, she said. You make yourself what you are. You make your own chances, your own luck.

How about ill people? I said. How about people who are born disabled?

That was due to their conduct in a former life.

So they were still responsible for their misfortunes? I asked.

Yes, she said. They were.

I asked her about people with brain tumours and if they were responsible for them. She felt that they probably were, due to their negative thinking and not being in a good place.

But don't we all die, I asked her. No matter how positive we think.

Maybe not, she said.

Then she told me that she had been touring in New Zealand once, and the stress of all the performing had taken its toll on her, and she just needed a massage. So she called a masseur, and he came to the apartment she was renting, and he gave her a back massage and she felt somewhat better for that. But a few more concerts, and the pains came back. So she called him again.

This time, during the course of the massage, he asked if she might be interested in any 'additional services' which he sometimes offered. She got angry at this, because the masseur had already told her that he was married.

'What about your wife?' she said.

But he just said that his wife was in the same line of business.

She told him to go. So he went.

She related this story to me with some heat and indignation, but I didn't see why. What, after all, did she expect? She had asked him back a second time to a place that she lived in on her own. He maybe thought that what he was offering was what she wanted – her whole object in asking him back?

By now most of the reading lights were out in the cabin and many of the screens were dark. Being a trained singer she had good voice projection and as a result maybe talked a little loud. Just as she began to tell me something else, a woman leapt to her feet four rows away and came down the aisle.

'Can't you keep your voice down?' she demanded. 'There are people here trying to sleep.'

Without waiting for an answer, she returned to her seat.

The opera singer made a face.

'I guess we'd better keep it down,' she said.

The conversation petered out. She didn't ask me one question about myself. But then performers seldom do.

As I was dozing off, I became aware of the acrobat on my right, moving in her seat.

'You want to get out?' I asked, getting ready to move. But she smiled and shook her head, indicating I should stay put. Then she stood up on the armrest, hopped over me to the next one, hopped over the opera singer and landed on her toes in the aisle.

She returned to her seat more or less the same way, just in reverse.

It must be good to have skills in life that actually come in useful.

When I got to Singapore I discovered that I didn't have the necessary visa to let me fly on to Australia. But a man at the boarding gate got me one online, for forty dollars. Some people restore your faith in human nature, and usually while the opposition are simultaneously undermining it.

For this leg of the journey I had an aisle seat, but when I arrived at it, I found someone sitting there.

'Excuse me, but I think that might be my seat.'

I showed the woman my ticket.

'Yes,' she said. 'I have a ticket for this seat here.' And she pointed at the one on the inside. 'Maybe you might prefer to sit there.'

'No thanks,' I said. 'I'll stick with mine.'

Reluctantly and with ill grace she moved, conveying with looks and muttering that I was not a gentleman.

When I told Louis about it, he said, 'You should have sat on her lap.'

But he was always there with the lateral thinking. Though I don't know that the seatbelt would have gone around us both.

22

GOOD NEWS

I had to clear the books out and empty the wardrobes of paint-spattered T-shirts and ragged shorts. There was little fiction on the shelves. Louis seldom read it. Out of his collection of hundreds of books, maybe ten were novels. The rest were technical, or how-tos – how to build a boat, a canoe, a xylophone, a guitar, a table; how to work with stained glass, how to do metalwork, how to take an engine apart; how to build a house from straw bales.

And then there were the biographies of men who had sailed oceans in home-made dinghies, or who had lived on crofts, or walked up Everest in their old shoes. And there were books on Zen and Buddhism. He had eclectic interests, he just didn't like made-up stories much, and why did he have to? Why should anyone? It's all lies anyway.

And while much fiction is said to contain some inner and relevant truth of how life is, a lot of it doesn't, and just holds many false depictions of reality. Not that there's anything wrong with escapism – until escapism is all you've got.

In books, there are the men who solve the cases and fathom the clues and bring order and justice to the world, and while they know how to take a beating and even a brief hospitalisation, they always make a comeback and are ready to go to work again in up-and-coming sequels. And while it's good to read about them every now and again, they don't seem to square with anybody you meet while you sit in the hospital waiting area, and the consultant still hasn't seen you yet, though your appointment was for an hour ago.

The guys who walk down the mean streets and solve the cases never have those problems. They deal with the things that fiction can fix. And that doesn't include tumours.

I was bagging things up and putting them out on the deck, prior to throwing them into the back of the ute and driving to the dump.

The front half of the Queenslander house was rented from Bella by a young couple, Tony and Beth. They had a yappy dog that Tony was always shouting at, telling it to be quiet and to behave itself. Tony was taciturn and unfathomable and sometimes surly. Louis believed he had offended him somehow, but I think he just didn't know what to say to him.

So I was out on the veranda and suddenly there was

Tony, out on his veranda too, right next to me. It would have been impolite to ignore him, so I said,

'Hi.'

'Hi,' he said.

'Just clearing stuff out here,' I said.

'Right,' he said.

'Holiday today?' I asked, for it was mid-morning on a weekday and he usually worked. He put up and took down For Sale boards for estate agents. Or he turned them into Under Offer boards. Or Sold boards. Though he told me once that his heart and ambitions lay in aircraft maintenance, only it was too late for that. But as he was still in his twenties, I couldn't exactly see why, but maybe didn't know enough.

'No,' he said. 'I'm taking the day off. Beth's inside. We're very upset.'

'Oh?'

'Tykie got run over last night.'

'What?'

'Nobody's fault. He slipped the lead and ran out into the road. The driver was upset too, but it wasn't his fault.'

'I'm sorry. I'm really sorry.'

'We loved that little creature.'

Really? I thought. Because you shouted at it a lot. But maybe we all shout a lot at the creatures we love.

'Well, I'm very sorry to hear that, Tony.'

'I mean, I know it's not like losing a brother—'

'No, no – it's still – you know – a living thing.'

'Anyway, we're taking the day off.'

'Of course.'

'I'd better go in and see how Beth's doing.'

169

'Yes, of course. Sure.'

He went inside. I carried on bagging things up and putting them out on the deck in boxes and carrier bags. Things for the Salvation Army to the left; stuff for the tip to the right.

As I brought some more books out, I heard footsteps. Two women, one middle-aged, one slightly younger, were filing up the steps to the veranda. I noticed that they were each carrying thick books with black leather covers. They were well but soberly dressed. They had a healthy, wholesome look about them. They were well-fed verging on plump, but by no means obese.

'Good morning,' the middle-aged one said as they advanced. 'We're here this morning with the Good News and—'

'Can I stop you right there?' I said. 'This isn't a good time, I'm afraid. My brother just died and I'm clearing out his house here, as I have to go home soon.'

They held their Bibles tightly. Maybe this contingency hadn't happened before as they did their rounds, spreading the Good News and the pamphlets and telling anyone receptive enough to listen all about Jesus.

'Oh, I'm so sorry,' the older woman said, and it seemed she probably did most of the talking and the other one was there for observation and back-up. 'We're very sorry for your loss. Maybe we could call back another time.'

If she says she's going to pray for me, I thought, I'm going to lose it.

She didn't. She just turned and they retreated back down the stairs.

But they hadn't finished yet. They walked along the path

170

and came up the stairs to Tony and Beth's place, and they tapped upon the door.

'Look, I . . .' I started to say. But something stopped me. I don't know what.

They tapped on the door a second time and Tony came to open it. He didn't look so great – stubbled and even hung-over.

'Yes?'

'Good morning,' the same woman said, and they both gave him smiles. 'We are here today to spread the Good News. Have you heard that Christ is risen and that—'

'Our dog got killed last night,' Tony said. 'It was run over by a truck. No one's fault. It just happened.'

The two women looked embarrassed, but more than that, a little suspicious too. They glanced across at me, maybe looking for signs of faint amusement and well-stifled laughter and guffaws. Perhaps they thought we'd seen them coming and had stitched the stories up between us. But, in the circumstances, they could scarcely call us liars.

So, 'We're so very sorry to hear that. So sorry for your loss. Maybe we can call again another time.'

The expression on Tony's face made the answer to that question a negative. He closed the door and went back inside.

The two women looked back across the veranda at me, and I think I maybe shrugged. Then down the stairs they went, and back out to the street, and they kept on walking. They didn't try any other of the neighbouring houses. Maybe they didn't think it would be a good idea. Maybe they didn't think it was worth their while.

Religion is something for the living. The dead already know the truth. Faith isn't something they need now. They have the hard facts. They just don't come back to tell us, that's all.

23

MASKS

Louis was going frantic, looking for something.
'What is it, Louis?'
'It's the bits and pieces.'
'What have you lost?'
'The – bits and pieces.'
'Is it the cool bag?'
'It's the – you know – bits and pieces.'
'Which particular bits and pieces? Which ones?'
'You know. You know. The – bits and pieces.'
He got angrier, more frustrated.
'The drugs? Is it the drugs?'
'Yes. The bits and—'
'Which ones? The chemo?'
'No.'
'Anti-nausea?'

'No.'
'Anti-inflammatory?'
'No!'
'Eye drops?'
'No!'
'That's all, Louis. That's all.'
'No, no, no. The bits and pieces!'
We found the blue cool bag and upturned it. The blister packs fell out and the bottles and his mobile and his will.

'It's all here, Louis. Everything's here. What is it?'
Once, some years back, he had tried to explain to me what he did when he worked in chemistry.

'I solve problems,' he'd said. 'The sort of problems most people wouldn't even understand.'

'How about the problems that everyone does under-stand, Louis?' I'd asked him. 'Can you solve those?'

'Nobody can solve those,' he'd said. 'Or we wouldn't be in this mess.'

Louis had degrees and diplomas in things most people didn't begin to understand, but now the words wouldn't come, not even the simple ones.

'Let's try again. From the beginning. What do you think you've lost?'

'The – damn it, I'm so stupid, so bloody stupid—'

'Louis, it's just a bad day, that's all. Sometimes you remember, sometimes you don't.'

'It's the – bits and pieces!'

'Is it the drugs?'

'Yes, yes.'

'Then what have we missed? Let me see the sheet.'

I took the drug sheet out of his bag and starting reading through it.

'Nausea, chemo, inflammatory, eye drops – steroids?'

'Steroids!'

'Okay. They're here. They're in the bottle. There. They're right here.'

He took the bottle and couldn't unscrew the childproof cap.

'Damn it!'

'It's all right. Here—'

'Damn it!'

'You want a glass of water?'

'Cuppa tea. Cuppa tea.'

'Okay. I'll fill the kettle.'

'What are we doing?'

'Just sit down, Louis. I'll make some tea.'

He took the steroids and drank the tea. I put on a DVD we'd bought at the supermarket. A moody and dark-lit spy thriller adapted from a famous novel. It was highly acclaimed, all about the British establishment and a spy service peopled by ex-public schoolboys and Oxbridge graduates, with whom it was hard to have much sympathy, though they anguished in their privilege.

When the film was over, Louis said,

'I didn't get a lot of that.'

'Me neither,' I said. 'And I'm still supposed to have all my brains.'

He gave me a doubtful look.

'I'll get a shoot-em-up next time,' I said.

'Get Liam Neeson,' he said. 'He did a good one about these guys who kidnap his daughter and he goes after them. But now there's a sequel and they're coming for him again, and this time it's his wife and his daughter they get.'

'Maybe, if there's another sequel, they'll come and get his cat,' I suggested.

'Liam doesn't take any crap,' Louis said.

'Okay. Let's go to Blockbuster and rent it, if they've got it in.'

Sometimes it isn't subtlety you want. It's someone who sorts things out and doesn't take any crap. We forgot about everything for over a hundred minutes. It was money well spent.

They kept Louis' fencing mask round at the radiation department. When the radiotherapy course was finished, they gave it to him to take home as a souvenir, or in case it might be needed again.

It just looks like a fencing mask. It's really a clamp. It's tailor-made to fit the patient's head and to hold it in place while the large radiation machine loops around and bombards the selected area of the brain with radiation. You don't want to go radiating the good part of the brain – instead of fixing tumours, you'd be causing them.

You lie on a flat bed. The mask goes over your head. The nurse clamps it into place, and you're held rigid. You wouldn't get the mask off on your own. You're imprisoned. It isn't an experience for the claustrophobic. I asked a nurse how they dealt with those who were. 'We talk to them,' she said.

Some masks are so large they don't just cover the head, they come down over the neck and shoulders, and even the whole chest. They are made of some kind of rigid white plastic and mesh.

You see people wandering around the waiting room, carrying their masks with them, like bit-part actors from some strange Japanese play. And then they get called, and they're on, and away they go to make their appearance.

There are all kinds of tumours and nobody wants any of them. But some are curable and some are not, and the purpose of the treatment is not to cure those, but to prolong remaining life. But whether the quality of that life prolonged is worth the struggle and the pain is an individual matter; it's a decision you need to make for yourself.

The doctors will usually advise you to have the treatment. They don't want to be sued. But their treatment is formulaic, and they dare not deviate from standard procedures, for fear of the lawyer's writ again. It makes you think of old-time medical men, with their cupping and their leeches. The point isn't necessarily whether the treatment does a whole lot of good, the point is that it is accepted by the medical profession. No one is going to criticise you for following the accepted medical path.

Tumours of the brain come in various sorts – some primary, some secondary. They can travel into the brain from other parts of the body, but do not go the other way. A primary brain tumour will not travel outwards and cause trouble elsewhere. It could, eventually, given sufficient time, but it doesn't get it.

Primary brain tumours come in four basic kinds and are graded accordingly. The most serious is a glioblastoma multiforme, a grade four. That was what Louis had. They are slightly more prevalent in men than women. No one knows what causes them, though there are indications that the causes could be genetic and/or environmental and could be due to exposure to certain chemicals, at some point in the past. Louis had worked in an asbestos mine and in other branches of the chemical industry. But who knows? People who've never even seen an asbestos mine still get them – the way people who've never smoked a cigarette in their lives still get lung cancer.

Why is it that we aren't afraid of death all the time, but only when its imminence is announced? We know what's going to happen. We know there is no choice. Yet when we hear it knocking it always comes as a terrifying surprise, a shock, an injustice. We all have to face it, but it's hard to be brave. The only way to go on is to pretend it won't happen.

Louis' radiation mask was there on the bookcase. I didn't want to keep it, but I didn't feel it was right to throw it away. But I did. What else could I do? Take it home in my hand luggage? Hang it on the wall, like some voodoo mask?

I drove the ute to the public dump and threw everything over the barrier and into the pile. I thought, there goes a life. One day all my personal effects and papers and the things of no use or value that I have hoarded far too long, they'll all go – things of little use and less beauty; books I kept without any intention of reading a second time.

We accumulate so much stuff, so many things, so many objects. There are so many items we just cannot seem to throw away, thinking that maybe they might come in handy, and sometimes they do, but mostly, they don't. They're just left there to bother our relatives and give them something to do to take their minds off things.

When our mother got old, Louis had her to come and live with him – in which act he had my admiration, as she would have driven me insane in two days. She died of a stroke, four years later.

Louis had kept all her belongings in boxes in the basement. So there were two batches of personal effects to get rid of. All her plates and cutlery were there, her chocolate-box pictures and her black and white photographs of unspecified relations from decades ago; her rosary and her crucifix and her picture of Jesus with a crown of thorns on his head and blood dripping down into his eyes that I remembered from childhood. A lot of Catholic homes are places adorned with grim reminders. I can think of few other religions whose central, abiding, defining image is that of a man in agony.

So it wasn't just Louis and his past I was throwing away, it was her too. Though I kept a little of each of them – some photographs, some small, personal possessions. It is strange to feel the potency of cheap material objects – things you wouldn't look at twice in a charity shop, were they not impregnated with the scent and the memories of your own past.

Maybe my son would like to have this pen, I thought; perhaps this bracelet would suit my daughter. But I knew that, really, the things were too old-fashioned and of another era. The new generations must look forwards. It is those who age and those who lose who look back.

In the end I got it all down to a suitcase for the hold

and a small piece of hand luggage. It all fitted into that. Two lives. There they were. Put together it was one hundred and forty-seven years of life. If I'd been a little more ruthless, I could have made do with the hand luggage alone.

The rest of it was all in my head – once-shared memories that I now shared with no one. I was the only one who survived now, who remembered the rented flats and the bed-and-breakfast places, who recalled the time Louis and I had to sleep in the bathroom, because we had no other space. All the cold and the making do and mean poverty that was part of so many lives then and no doubt still is. All the love and all the flashes of laughter. A classmate once told me that we lived in a slum. I hadn't known it until he said so. I'd thought we were fine.

There was nobody left to know. There was no other witness to all those ordinary, familiar, banal, dramatic, mundane, extraordinary, devastating events.

I remembered seeing my father in the back room of a pub into which children were allowed. There was a piano there. He sat down at it and began to play – fluently, easily. I'd never known he could play the piano and I never saw him do so again. But to whom is that even vaguely important now? Not Louis. Not anyone.

And so it must be with all lives, and all those who survive for a while longer. All our importances that mean so little to others – and all their recollections, so similar to our own, and yet which barely touch us, except in their evocation.

One and a half suitcases. I checked the hold luggage in at the bag-drop at the airport. The assistant asked me if I had packed the bag myself. Then she read out a list of prohibited articles, and I confirmed I did not have any of them in the case. The objects that it contained could do no harm to anyone.

24

MELON CLAW

My career as a Louis substitute was starting to take off and I was getting regular offers coming in for personal appearances, while I spent my daytimes emptying his wardrobes, clearing his junk, boxing his books for the Salvation Army and trying to dispose of the accumulated debris of half a lifetime.

Babs, Halley's sister, called and said,

'Derek is having a big birthday this weekend, and he's rented a place up in the mountains, and he's invited a load of people and he was going to ask Louis, but—'

I said I'd go.

It took three hours to get there. I went with Halley in Louis' ute – which would soon be Halley's ute, if the will copy ever got authorised – and he drove as he knew the way. We sped along with the window falling down and the fan on perpetual maximum.

'How about I put the radio on to blot the fan out?' Halley said.

'The radio doesn't work,' I told him.

'Okay,' he said. For he seemed the philosophical sort. Then he glanced at me sideways and said, 'She had a false plastic thumb then?'

'That's how she did the trick. Removing the clothes was all distraction and sleight of hand.'

'Sleight of hand with a plastic thumb. It kind of takes the magic away.'

'But it's nice to know how things are done.'

'Maybe,' he said. 'Or sometimes maybe not.'

'She was magic, anyway,' I reminded him, 'just standing there with nothing on.'

We drove on up through dripping rainforests and roads with layers of mist lying on them. Eventually we caught sight of Derek and Babs and Babs and Halley's mother in their car, and we tailed them.

Derek turned off up a track and we kept following. We drove another five miles or more and came to a farm.

'This is it,' Halley said. 'I think.'

Next to the farm was a so-called homestead, with a couple of bunk rooms and a couple of doubles. There were others already there, people Derek had invited. He introduced me and said I was Louis' brother, and they all seem satisfied with that.

We had a barbecue that night. The women were mostly tough and heavy smokers. Like Liam Neeson, they took no crap. We sat outside and knocked the cabernet sauvignon and the Little Creatures back.

Derek got a camp fire going, and some of us sat next to it, perched on stones, staring at the flames, wherein all mysteries were solved and all answers danced.

Halley's brother Charles had turned up, and he too was an artist who lived in a shed. His grey hair was in a ponytail and he wore charity-shop clothes, for being an artist does not always pay. In fact mostly it doesn't pay at all. It's really a kind of charity work in its own right.

The breeze blew the fire smoke into Charlie's eyes, but he didn't shift to get away from it. He just licked his thumb and then held his thumb out in front of him, and the smoke got the message, and it turned away and wafted in another direction.

Halley was watching this.

'That is such bullshit,' he said.

But Charles just gave him a thin smile, for the evidence spoke for itself.

'Such bullshit,' Halley said again. 'That is total crap.'

The wind turned again and this time the smoke blew into my eyes. I licked my thumb and held it up, but the smoke kept coming.

'What am I doing wrong, Charlie?'

'You're not convinced,' he said. 'You've got to believe in it or it won't work.'

'He's talking bullshit,' Halley said.

I was reassured to see that brothers are the same the world over, and have a tendency not to agree with each other, particularly on vital matters.

*

184

The next morning we had breakfast out on the big wooden table. The farmer's dogs appeared and hopped up on to the barbecue iron and licked all the taste and grease of last night's sausages from it.

'That is disgusting,' Babs said. 'We'll be cooking on that again later.'

'It'll burn off,' Derek told her.

A friend of Derek's had brought his boat and we were going to the lake to catch red claw, so I heard. Red claw being smallish freshwater lobsters. Derek had been on the internet and had assured himself by consulting various websites that the best bait to use was melon.

The rest of us thought this was a hoax of some kind, but it was Derek's birthday, so we went with it. We cut up melons and put them into crab pots, then went out to the lake and heaved them into the water.

Two hours later we returned to pull them up. Nothing. Just sliced melon. We moved the pots and came back another two hours later. Still no red claw but plenty of soggy melon. Same again another two hours after that. We were all feeling hungry by then, so we gave up on the red claw, reeled in the pots and returned to the homestead for a cheese sandwich.

There was serious snoring in the bunk house that night, possibly due to the intake of alcohol, though the most serious snorer, another of Derek's brother-in-laws, was a reformed drinker on the twelve-point plan, and all he'd had was Coca-Cola.

Halley and I went for a bike ride early the next morning, past fields of startled wallabies, who froze, watched us a moment, and then ran, bouncing away into the mist. We passed ruined homesteads of hand-hewn timber and corrugated roofs, long since deserted, built on patches of scrub where some subsistence farmer and his family might once have eked out a hard living.

When you stopped pedalling, there was no sound of vehicles, not even from far away, only the sounds of the breeze and of birds and other living things.

Don't tell me Louis would have liked this, I thought, because I already know.

'Louis would have liked it here,' Halley said.

'He would,' I agreed. 'He would.'

'Want to cycle back now?'

We did. The wallabies were back in the field, but on seeing us, they ran away again. When we got to the homestead the women were still at the breakfast table, smoking cigarettes and drinking tea. They were all substantial and in their middle years. If you'd asked them for a favour, they wouldn't have let you down.

Victor, the snorer, was mechanically minded, so I asked him to have a look at the ute and see if he could stop the fan constantly blowing on max, as I couldn't locate the fuse. He took half the dashboard apart, but he fixed it.

Halley and I were able to drive back in relative peace.

I thanked Derek for the invitation, but he was lying on a sofa, looking hung-over and morose, as if the passing of his significant birthday had brought intimations of mortality with it which he had hitherto managed to ignore.

We cleaned and tidied the place up and threw the melons into the compost bin. There were so many empty wine bottles we took some of them back with us from shame. Then we all drove away in our various directions.

It was a good weekend. I got back to Louis' place quite late and it was cold and empty and the traces of him were going as, little by little, I was taking them away.

I found a Little Creature hiding in the fridge and I tried to prise the cap off with my thumb, as I had seen done. But I didn't have the knack and so used an opener.

Up in the roof the possums were moving. Maybe they were rooting away, maybe they were just getting comfortable. After all, they'd have known each other some time now, and it can't be passionate sex every night, not even for possums.

I thought of all the strange and unexpected places life will take you to, and the ones that death will take you to as well, and the people you meet along the way who you otherwise would never have known.

I thought how strange and wonderful the world was, and how both sad and beautiful life had been, and then I thought it was maybe the beer thinking and not me.

I went and stood in Louis' room. I could have slept in his bed, had I wanted to, but I didn't. I put the light out, and went and lay on my own.

Who, I wondered, do I most wish was here right now?

But I found that it was a question not easily answered.

All I saw were dancing shapes on the wall, as the tree branches out in the garden waved in the moonlight, and then I fell asleep, and when I awoke, the telephone was ringing.

I hurried to answer it, and it was my wife, and she said, 'How are you? How are you feeling?'

I said, 'I'm okay. I'm managing. How are you?'

'I'm okay,' she said. 'We're all fine here.'

187

And the sun came up, and the day started, though where she was, it was night time, and the light was coming to its end.

25

DICTATION

'You'll write it all down, won't you?' Louis said to me.

'If that's what you want, I'll try to,' I said.

'It's what you do, isn't it?'

'I try to, Louis, but it doesn't always work. If you want to know the truth, most of the time it doesn't work. I got lucky with a few things and made enough money to keep going, but most of the time it doesn't work. I know I've got a wife and kids and a house and a car and a pension scheme and we get the food at Waitrose, but inside, I'm a bohemian.'

'Well, you can make it work.'

'I can't know that, Louis, but I'll try.'

'And no crap,' he said. 'No sentimental stuff and no crap. The world's full of crap and there's already too much of it.

It doesn't matter how it is, just as long as it's not full of crap.'

'I can't make any promises, Louis. Why don't you, you know, get something down now?'

'I can't even write a shopping list now.'

Which was true. He had trouble signing his name.

Four days after the surgeon had cut a substantial part of Louis' brain out, Louis decided that he would walk home from the hospital. He managed the first two miles without incident, but then he felt immensely tired and had to sit down on a bench. He passed out and woke up two hours later, then continued on his way.

I guess the people who saw him sleeping there would have thought him to be a vagrant, or a rough sleeper, with maybe an alcohol problem. He had the wild beard, the mad eyebrows and the tattered clothes for the part. They would not have imagined him to be a graduate of prestigious universities, who had travelled widely, conversed in several languages, who had solved problems that others did not even know were problems, as they could not understand the question, let alone the answer to it.

Louis had been up on his feet the day after the operation.

'I'm not one to stay in bed,' he told me down the phone. 'You see some of them in here, they've already given up. I've been walking round the hospital and down to Starbucks and I went outside a while too. I've lost a few pounds, but nothing serious. Don't know what'll happen with the steroids, but right now, I'm at fighting weight.'

Once home, he cycled to the supermarket on his bike

for groceries. But he nearly had an accident. The operation had damaged his peripheral vision. He stopped cycling. He got scared of running into someone.

The day I got there, he took me for a three-mile walk. He tripped and fell on a kerb, and lay a while on the pavement.

'Are you okay, Louis?'

'I'm so stupid,' he said. 'I didn't see it coming.'

'Don't get up yet, just wait a minute.'

A car drew up and the window slid down.

'You okay there? Can I help? You need a lift? Is he all right? I saw what happened.'

'We're all right,' Louis growled. 'We don't need any help, thank you. We can manage on our own.'

I thanked the motorist and he drove on. Louis got to his feet and I saw that his leg was bleeding.

'Louis, we should have taken the lift. Are you all right?'

'I'm fine,' he said. 'I'm fine.'

'Let's turn back then.'

'No. I'm going to show you where everything is.'

So we walked on.

'You sure about this, Louis? You sure you're all right?'

'We're tough,' he said. 'We're tough.'

26

THE WAY

Kirstin called and asked if I would like to see her house, which was a three-hour drive away, up in the outback.

'Louis helped build it,' she said.

So I said I would. She asked Halley too, whom she'd known a long time. She'd sold her art and he had sold his picture frames at the same country markets.

We left about nine one morning in Kirstin's Hyundai. She asked me to drive, and she sat in the back, and Halley sat in the front next to me, and we headed north out of the city.

As we drove a large, white, new-looking car overtook us. It was a Lexus or something like that and it bore a personalised number-plate, the first three letters of which were ZEN.

'Look at that,' I said. 'How can that be?'

'What?' Halley said.

'How can it be Zen to have a ZEN number-plate?'

'Maybe they're initials,' Kirstin said. 'Maybe it's Zachariah Emmanuel Norman.'

'Possibly,' I agreed, 'but unlikely in my opinion. I think it's some teacher of Buddhism or something, trying to bring in the business.'

'So you think advertising Zen is not very Zen?' Halley said.

'No. How can it be? Surely the way of Zen is the way of non-attachment to material things, which would include personalised number-plates, wouldn't it? If your ego is telling you that you need to tell everybody how Zen you are, then you're not Zen at all. It's a contradiction in terms.'

'But maybe,' Halley said, 'you can get too attached to non-attachment. You could get so attached to non-attachment that it becomes a form of ego in itself. And so, to show that you are not overly attached to non-attachment, you get a personalised number-plate. Because to deliberately and calculatedly avoid personalised number-plates, in order to demonstrate to the world that you are not a personalised number-plate kind of guy and above such things, would be a form of attachment even worse than having one.'

'You mean it's "The Way of the Number-Plate"?'

'Something like that.'

'I think whoever was driving that car was a bullshit artist,' I said.

'Then maybe he's trying to achieve enlightenment through "The Way of the Bullshit",' Halley said.

'There seems to be a lot of people taking that route,' I said. 'So tell me, if you wanted to find out about Zen Buddhism, would you go and study under a guy who drove a big white Lexus and had a personalised number-plate with ZEN on it?'

'Maybe. Maybe not,' Halley said. 'But I wouldn't rule it out completely.'

'Can you make smoke change direction by licking your thumb?' I asked him.

'I'm working on it,' he said.

'Left here,' Kirstin said.

So we turned left and changed the subject.

On we drove. In the car with us we had a loaf of bread, a large fish, and a bottle of wine. For some reason it made me think of Jesus. We also had some tomatoes, salad leaves, a bottle of water and some Little Creatures. Everything except the bread was in an eskie.

The journey got tedious, but after a time we left the highway and took a minor road which led through tumbleweed towns and past hedgeless fields of scrub. Then we drove alongside cultivated land, with huge irrigation devices upon it, past orchards and green crops and massive greenhouses, and there were fruit pickers at work in the merciless sun, wearing hats with long drapes at the back of them, to protect their necks from the burning heat.

'They immigrants?' I asked Kirstin.

'Mostly,' she said. 'Some backpackers too, making a little money, or staying on the farms and doing it for keep.'

On we went. The land seemed eternal to someone like

me from a small island. On and on it continued, as far as you could see, until it went out of focus in a blur of heat. As we drove there were mirages hovering about the road, promising water that was never there when you got to where it should have been.

'And left here now too.'

We turned off the road and on to a single lane dirt track. It ran over gullies and bridges and by creeks and woodland. Here there were acres of burnt and blackened trees, petrified by old fires and yet to recover and issue green shoots. We passed burning grass and a fire engine and some men beating out small flames.

'It hasn't rained for two months here,' Kirstin said.

'You worry about fire?' Halley asked her.

'I can't do much about it,' she said.

We drove on for miles, the Hyundai taking a battering. Red dust rose up into the air behind us, and advertised where we were. We saw the occasional homestead, but there weren't many, and they appeared deserted.

'How long have you had the place here?'

'I bought the land twenty years ago,' Kirstin said. 'When I got divorced.'

'How much?' Halley said.

'Seventeen thousand.'

'How many acres?'

'I don't know – forty?'

Halley whistled.

'And then?'

'My son's an engineer and he designed the house and I had some help and built it. But now I'm looking to sell. I'm getting older and need to be closer to the city.'

'How far's your nearest shop?' I asked her.

'Nine miles,' she said.

'Long way to go for the newspaper.'

'I don't bother with them too much.'

We passed more scorched and blackened fields. There were koalas in the gum trees and wallabies standing by the tree margin watching us pass, indifferent, barely curious. Galahs and parakeets were in the treetops, screeching at the rising dust.

'Had any viewers? How long's it been on the market?' Halley asked.

'Eighteen months and two viewings. One offer.'

'Not enough?'

'They offered to take it for nothing,' she said. 'They were old hippies and had no money, but they felt that they were in tune with the place, and if I let them have it for nothing, they'd look after it.'

'Give your home a good home, huh?'

There was a ramshackle house ahead of us and a gate blocking the track.

'My neighbour,' Kirstin said. 'He'll open it.'

Two men sat in the yard. One was in his seventies, one was in his forties, and he didn't look right. They sat on old chairs and between them they had a crate of beer and an ice box. The son looked vacant or stoned and the old man had a shotgun on his knee.

'Friendly looking,' Halley said.

The old man got up and opened the gate for us to drive through.

'Thank you,' Kirstin called. He saluted her with his beer

can. Halley and I thanked him too, just to be on the safe side.

We drove on and he closed the gate behind us, then he sat back down and opened another beer.

'What do they do all day?' Halley said.

'What they're doing,' Kirstin said. 'And there's a few chickens around the place, and some veg growing.'

'What's going to happen when the old man dies and the son's left on his own with the beer and shotgun?' Halley said.

Kirstin shrugged.

'Hopefully I'll be gone by then.'

'Is there any other way of accessing your property?'

'No.'

'You think maybe pappy and junior back there are the reason you're not getting too many offers?'

'They're fine,' Kirstin said. 'Never been a problem with me. He usually asks me to stop and have a beer, but I say I'm busy.'

'Right,' Halley said. 'Okay.'

But he sounded dubious.

And then we were there. We pulled off the track and parked under shade. The house was built into the side of a hill, its veranda held up by timbers, its back part resting on foundations. It was cool and elegant, but comprised only one room. You opened the door and there you were, everything faced you, living room, bedroom, kitchen, all in one, with only a screen for privacy, should you want some.

'A drink?'

There was lemonade in the fridge, which was powered

by solar panels, and there was a generator in an out-house for back-up if needed.

Next to the house was a studio, also built in wood, with an apexed roof.

'Louis used it as a workshop,' Kirstin said. 'Originally it was my studio, but I didn't use it any more.'

'Why did you give up?' I asked her.

'It gave me up,' she said.

Behind the house the land rose into the woods. The gradient was so steep that when you tried to climb up, your feet slid underneath you, and you had to scramble, leaning forwards, using your hands as well as your feet, walking like an ape.

After we'd seen the view, we came back down and drank beer on the veranda, looking down into the valley and the creek and where – when the rain came – there was a swimming hole and cool bathing and fresh water.

'What do you do for drinking water?' Halley asked.

'Bore hole,' she said. 'And the rain-water tanks last forever. I don't use much.'

Then there was a sudden loud and ominous rumbling. 'What is that?'

We went round to the back of the house. The noise was boiling water. The day was so hot and the sun had been on the solar panels so long that the water in the reservoir tank was boiling. The pressure-relief valve had opened and vapour was hissing out, like steam from an old coal train.

'Never seen it do that before,' Kirstin said. 'Shall we go in and eat?'

We grilled the fish and laid the table and cut up the

bread and salad. When we had finished eating, Kirstin took out an album of photographs and showed them to me. They were of her and Louis building her house; of her and Louis on their trip up the coast, along the eastern seaboard to the Barrier Reef. She seemed a little wistful, and when Halley was out of the way for five minutes, looking at some wood she had that might do for his picture frames, Kirstin said,

'I thought about Louis a lot, you know, after we broke up. There was an incident, you know—'

'He told me there was something,' I lied. 'He never said what exactly.'

'But I felt I couldn't go back. Many times I thought about picking up the phone. But after the incident – I felt I couldn't risk that.'

I wondered about her ex-husband, and what kind of man he was.

'No,' I said. 'Well – I'm sorry.'

'But thank you for calling me,' she said. 'For including me.'

It was ten years since they'd broken up.

'Do you get lonely here?' I asked. 'Or doesn't it bother you?'

'Sometimes, but mostly I like it. I do some gardening, plant trees, read, cook. I've a television here and internet – it's slow, but it works – and I get visitors sometimes.'

'You really don't paint any more?'

'No,' she said.

'Are they yours, on the wall?'

'Yes,' she said.

'They're good.'

'Thanks. Louis built his canoe out there,' she said, going to the veranda and pointing at the studio.

'How'd he take it home?'

'On the back of his ute.'

'He ever use it?'

'Once or twice.'

Halley reappeared and Kirstin said she wanted to clear up and why didn't we go and look around, so we left her to it.

We followed the track about half a mile and found another house; it was haphazard and disorienting and like something from the Brothers Grimm. It adhered to no formal house plan known to architecture.

It was like the *Mary Celeste* – the ship found floating with no one on board, but with signs of very recent habitation.

The doors of the place were ajar, there were plates on the table, bright clothes on the line, knives and forks in the sink. Everything was dishevelled and falling apart.

'Who lives down the road?' Halley asked Kirstin when we got back.

'Some hippy types use it as a weekend place. They chill out and smoke dope. They don't bother me. They don't come by as often as they used to. I think they find the drive too much. They're getting old.'

We drank some coffee and then Kirstin said we maybe ought to move soon, before the light went, as it was a long drive back. We packed up our rubbish and took it with us.

Halley drove this time. When we got to the beer and shotguns place, there was no one there. I got out and opened the gate and then closed it behind us.

We rejoined the road and drove back south, the darkness chasing us and the neon coming on.

We passed a sign reading 'Small Animal Hospital Ahead'.

'Is that a small hospital for all animals, do you think?' I said. 'Or a hospital for small animals, and you shouldn't go round there with a large one?'

'The latter,' Halley said.

'So what if you've got a large animal and it needs attention?'

'You shoot it,' Halley said.

And that was the end of that conversation.

We got back towards Louis' place, but we were hungry again by then, so we headed for Tomato Brothers and ordered pizza. Kirstin rang her daughter who came over and joined us. She would spend the night there at her daughter's. It was too far to go back to her own house.

We stood outside the restaurant and said goodbye. Halley and I walked back to Louis' house, where Halley had left his ute, and he said he'd be in touch soon, and he got into his ute and started up the engine.

I went inside and sat at the table in Louis' kitchen, and it felt as if it had been a long day. But like all the other ones, short or long, it had ended. I tied the dongle to the bamboo pole and stuck it out of the window so I could check my e-mails.

I remembered an incident when I was very young, maybe seven or eight years old. I don't recall exactly what I was doing, but I knocked the salt cellar off the table and it smashed on the kitchen floor.

I was terrified of my father's anger and I went in search of Louis and told him what I'd done and how scared I was.

He was blasé about it. 'It'll be all right, just tell him,' he said.

'It won't be all right, Louis. He'll go mad. He'll kill me. Would you tell him you did it – please?'

He could have said no and let me stew, but he didn't. 'Sure.'

He went and found our father, who was unemployed at that time and sitting brooding in the sitting room over the last of his hand-rolling tobacco.

'Dad,' Louis said. 'I had a bit of an accident and knocked over the salt cellar and it broke. Sorry.'

'Don't worry. These things happen. Have you cleared it up?'

'Just going to.'

'I'll help,' I said.

Later, when we were in our beds, Louis said, 'See, I told you it would be all right.'

'It was only all right because it was you, Louis. If it had been me he would have killed me.'

'Nah.'

I was grateful to him, but I still believe it to be so – our father would forgive Louis things that were inexcusable in me, because Louis was so smart and bright, and he was going to carry the candle and fly the flag and do such wonderful things. But I was the second son who should have been a daughter, and was a disappointment from the start.

So I was truly grateful, but I was resentful too, and bitter, that I didn't get equal treatment.

But the past is done. It's over and finished.

So why then does it so often feel like a splinter never removed?

27

REPRISE

We went back to Jack and May's for dinner, as invited.

May had plainly been on the white wine since early afternoon, and Jack had also had a few – though maybe not as many.

'Louis! How lovely to see you!' she said. Though, in truth, it was getting harder to see him, as the beanie hat was getting lower on the forehead with each passing day. 'Have a drink.'

'Can't,' Louis said. 'My head.'

'Jack, maybe Louis would like an orange juice. Give his brother some wine.'

'I'm driving, I'm afraid.'

'You can have one, for God's sake.'

'May, don't force him—'

'I'm not forcing anyone, would I force anyone to have a drink? People can have a drink or not have a drink. You could have got a taxi over and then we could all have had a drink. But if you don't want a drink, well, then don't have one.'

We were party poopers. We sipped our orange juice. After some strained small talk, we sat down at the table.

'It's melon,' May said, in case we were unable to recognise it.

'Good bait for red claw apparently,' I said. But they weren't much interested.

'Jackie, would you top up my glass?'

After the melon there was a wait while the fish cooked. Jack decided to tell us a little about his theatre days, back when he was young, and could have turned professional if his nerve had held.

'So I was offered the lead part in this play. A Harold Pinter. Do you know Harold Pinter at all?'

We said that we did, by repute.

'Well, I was offered this part and—'

May emitted a groan.

'What is it, dear?'

'Not the Harold Pinter anecdote,' she said. 'Not again.'

'Is there a problem, dear?'

'I've only heard it about thirty-five thousand times, that's all. I probably know it off by heart and word for word.'

'But Louis and his brother haven't heard it, dear. They might be interested—'

'Oh, well, you tell it then. Don't worry about me. I've only heard it about thirty-five thousand times. But never mind. I'm sure I can sit through it once more.'

I looked across the table at Louis. He seemed oblivious, as if his beanie hat provided a kind of sanctuary and rendered unpleasant things invisible and inaudible.

'Then maybe another time,' Jackie said. 'When it's more appropriate.'

We changed the subject. May scooped the plates up and went into the kitchen with them. She was wearing a lot of jewellery and it rattled against the crockery. The door to the kitchen remained open.

'Can I help, dear?'

'No.'

Jackie told us of some other aspects of his theatrical life. While he did so, strange noises emanated from the kitchen. He paused and called.

'May, are you all right in there?'

The noises stopped and May appeared in the threshold, her glass in her hand and her apron around her waist. She appeared to be wearing some kind of flapper-style dress under it, preserved from the 1920s.

'Of course I'm all right. Why wouldn't I be all right?'

'You seemed to be talking to yourself, dear.'

'Talking to myself? I was singing, actually. I was *singing*!'

'Oh, I see, yes, right.'

'But if it doesn't meet with your high standards, then excuse me for doing so. Pardon me for opening my mouth. Pardon me for singing to myself. Pardon me!'

Then she disappeared to put the fish on the plates.

'You mustn't mind May,' Jackie said. 'She's always being herself.'

'Who else would I bloody be?' her voice asked, from off.

'More orange juice?' Jackie asked.

'Give 'em a proper drink!' May shouted.

'They're driving, dear.'

'What? All of them?'

'And Louis has had an operation.'

'Louis house-sits for us. Did he tell you? He's marvellous with the cats.'

She came in with breaded fish. She had thawed it out earlier and put it under the grill. It was accompanied with baked potatoes and severely boiled broccoli.

'Are you at all familiar with the plays of a writer called Simon Gray?' Jackie asked, as we got stuck into the fish.

I conceded that I did know a little about him.

'Well, when I was starting off, and when I could actually have turned professional, I was offered the lead in—'

'Yes,' May butted in. 'We were supposed to be going on honeymoon too, weren't we?'

'It was too good an opportunity to miss, dear.'

'Supposed to be going on honeymoon, but no. He takes on a six-week run in a play. That was our honeymoon.'

'It was such a good opportunity, dear—'

'And when we finally did get to go off on honeymoon, what then? Yes.'

Jackie looked somewhat uncomfortable.

'We had to take your drug-addicted cousin along with us, didn't we, to keep him off the stuff.'

'There was nobody else able to help, dear, and it was a difficult time for the family—'

'That was our honeymoon – three of us. Three of us on honeymoon, all going off together, Jackie here, and me, and a raging drug addict, to make up the threesome. And that – and *that* – was our honeymoon.' She took a swallow of wine. 'But anyway,' she said. 'How are you keeping, Louis? How's the head?'

'I'm fine, thanks, May,' Louis said.

No one appeared to think there was anything out of the ordinary going on here, except me, and even I was beginning to question my judgement. Maybe this was average dinner-table behaviour and I was just a pommie prude and stuck-up bastard.

'That was lovely, thanks,' I said, leaving most of the leathery fish and dried-out spud on my plate, half-hidden under the soggy broccoli.

'There's pudding,' May said, in a tone that could merely have been informative, or which might have been a threat.

The table was cleared and she disappeared again for a while. Jackie told us some more amateur theatrical stories, about his triumphs on the boards and how he had received offers to turn professional, but how that profession was too insecure for a man with a mortgage and a wife.

'There's pudding,' May said, making a grand entrance – every entrance she made had a certain grandeur to it, along with an element of unsteadiness. 'And there's some Rocky Road.'

She put shop-bought apple pies down in front of us, along with a bowl of her famous confectionery.

'You like Rocky Road, don't you, Louis?'

'You can't beat May's Rocky Road,' Louis said.

'You can take some home with you if we don't eat it all.'

I thought of the bag of Rocky Road sitting in the fridge

at Louis' place, just lurking in there getting ready to break your teeth.

'There. Pudding, pudding, pudding.' She dealt the bowls out. 'Help yourselves to whatever else. I've had enough. I'm going to bed.'

'Oh, are you off to bed, dear?'

'I've had enough,' May said. 'I've had enough of everything.'

And then, with a sparkling smile and undeniable charm, she turned the radiance of her personality upon us and said, 'Louis, so nice to see you again, and so nice to meet your brother, and I do hope you get well soon, and do take some Rocky Road. I'm off to bed. Goodnight.'

And she left.

We ate our puddings. Jack did not appear unduly embarrassed or especially mortified.

'That's May,' he said. 'She's like that. We've had twelve to dinner and she's gone to bed.' ('With all of them?' I almost said, but exercised restraint.) 'It's just her way. More orange juice?'

There was the clatter of descending footsteps.

'Are you talking about me?'

'I was just telling Louis and his brother about Harold Pinter, dear.'

'Oh, God. I must have heard that twenty thousand times.'

'Thirty-five thousand, dear.'

'I can't get this necklace off, Jackie. Be a dear. Be a dear, Jackie, and unclip my necklace for me.'

To make things easier for him, she knelt down in front of him on the floor, a little like that picture of Mary Queen of Scots at her execution, as she prepared to have her head chopped off.

'So I am good for something then, dear?' Jackie said affectionately, reaching for the catch.

She turned and gave him a long and penetrating look.

'I suppose so,' she said at length. 'But not much.'

Finally the long-suffering Jack took offence.

'Then maybe I won't unclip your necklace for you. Maybe I won't.'

'Then don't,' May said, struggling up on to one knee. 'I'll just pull the fucking thing off then and chuck it on the fucking floor.'

Jack removed the necklace for her. She took it in her hand, stood, flashed us another lipstick-smeared smile and said again, 'Lovely to have met you. Don't rush away on my account. Jackie will make you some coffee. Night, night.'

And back up the stairs she went.

Jack seemed largely unabashed.

'That's May,' he said. 'She has her ways. Coffee?'

We stayed another thirty minutes, listening to Harold Pinter anecdotes. Louis finally cited tiredness and an early start tomorrow for chemo and radiotherapy.

'Do call in again,' Jackie said.

And we finally got out of the place.

As we drove off in the ute, I turned to Louis and said, 'Are they always like that?'

'She's a character, May, isn't she?' Louis said. 'They're nice people, aren't they?'

We drove on in silence. Then Louis said,

'I forgot the Rocky Road.'

'You want to go back for it?' I asked him.

'Maybe not,' he said.

'Probably wise,' I said.

'Left here,' Louis said, and he raised his hand, and pointed right.

I thought to myself, *And people go to art galleries for surrealism. Like they couldn't get all that at home.*

Terri, who knew both May and Jack, told me later that the major problem was that all Jack's friends were homosexuals, and that when it came to being married, his heart wasn't in it, and that was the reason why May started opening wine bottles at ten past two in the afternoon. But you can't build a case on rumours.

I never saw either May or Jackie again. I rang to tell them that Louis had died, but they didn't pick up, so I left a message. Then I rang again to tell them the time and place of the funeral, but they didn't get back to me and didn't appear.

I worked my way through the contacts list in Louis' mobile and through the scraps of paper that constituted his address book. I found a number for a guy called Wanday, and I saw that cheques had been made out to him too, for a charity he ran for a free Tibet.

I sent him a text message and he called and said he would be at the crematorium. But he wasn't there. The day after I got a call from him asking where everybody was. 'I'm at the crematorium,' he said. 'And the place is deserted.'

There'd been a mix-up and the day and the date had got confused. I apologised and so did he. He said not to worry and that was the end of the conversation. We never did meet.

I mentioned this to Halley and said that maybe Wanday

should change his name to Wrongday. He didn't think it particularly funny, or even in good taste. Maybe he was right. But you have to try and keep your spirits up the best and only ways you can.

28

NO DRAMAS

The integral DVD player in the TV stopped working and we couldn't watch the shoot-em-ups any more.
'It's no good,' Louis said. 'We're screwed.'
'Louis, I thought you told me the set was nearly new. Where's the receipt?'
'Be in the bag, if anywhere.'
I looked in the clear plastic bag containing the instruction manual, and there I found the receipt, but two months old, along with a document he had paid extra for, called the 'No Hassles, No Lemons Guarantee'.
'Louis, the receipt's here and it looks like you also paid for some additional warranty. It's just a matter of taking the set back.'
'It won't be that easy.'
'I don't see why not.'

'Because it isn't. Because we're screwed.'

'Louis, it's just your frame of mind.'

The next day, after the radiotherapy, we came back to the house. Louis was too tired to go to the shop, so he crashed out for a few hours, and I said I'd do it.

I put the TV in the ute, and armed with a map and the No Lemons warranty, I set off to the white goods' store.

It was one of those huge electrical warehouses and it turned out to be the place we had got the fridge and washing machine.

I carried the TV inside and put it down upon the central counter.

'How are you today?' the girl asked.

'Fine,' I said. 'Can I see someone about this TV?'

'Chris is with a customer just now, but he'll be right over.'

Chris' customer proved to be of the time-consuming kind.

'I'm sorry about the wait,' the girl said, 'but he won't be much longer, I'm sure.'

'You can't deal with it?'

'Not my department, I'm afraid.'

My patience got stretched. But after twenty minutes, the customer left, and Chris came over.

'This gentleman here, Chris,' the girl said. 'He's been waiting.'

'Hi. How are you today?' Chris said.

'Fine,' I lied.

'So what's the problem?' Chris said, and he seemed to be keeping cheerful.

214

'It's this set,' I said. 'My brother bought it from you eight weeks ago, but the DVD player has stopped working. I have the receipt here and there's also this warranty and—'

'You've tried other DVDs?'

'We have tried plenty of DVDs. It plays none of them. Or they get stuck in there and they don't come out until the following morning.'

'You mind if I try?'

'Not at all.'

He plugged in the TV, got a DVD and inserted it. It got stuck.

'It doesn't seem to be working.'

'That's why I'm here.'

'Okay. Well, let me see what we can do about that.'

He took a look on the computer.

'All right. We can exchange that for you, not a problem, except that I see that your set is now discontinued and we don't have any. The new model is in stock though, and we can let you have that.'

'Fine.'

'That'll just be another fifty dollars.'

I felt my heart thump.

'Excuse me?'

'Just another fifty dollars.'

'For what?'

'For the new set.'

'No,' I said. 'Just wait a minute. You sold my brother a TV set. The set does not work. Therefore you replace it. At no cost.'

'Ah, but that set is no longer available,' Chris said.

'That,' I told him, 'is not my problem. That is your

problem. I don't live in this country. But I don't imagine that your consumer laws here are a whole lot different. That TV is not fit for purpose. It is not of merchantable quality. So you need to replace it. At no cost.'

'We can't do that, sir,' Chris said. 'Because that model has been superseded.'

'Not,' I said, 'my problem. Either you replace this set, or you refund the money.'

'The set is two months old.'

'And it's not working.'

'I'll tell you what else we can do, sir. We can get this set fixed.'

'Okay . . .' I was doubtful.

'Only I do need to warn you that we'll have to send it away. That could take up to three months.'

'Three months?'

'Up to three months.'

'Let me tell you something, Chris. My brother has a brain tumour. He can no longer read. Listening to music and watching DVDs are two things he can do. In three months he might be dead, Chris. I don't feel we can wait that long.'

'It is fifty dollars for the new set, sir, and then—'

'Excuse me. Excuse me, Chris. May I read you something?'

'I'm sorry, sir?'

'May I? It's just there, by the receipt. I brought it with me but you're leaning on – thank you. Can I read you this? My brother paid an extra sixty dollars for it. It says, No Hassles, No Lemons. Your shop logo on the front there. No Hassles, No Lemons Guarantee. Right?'

'The thing is, sir—'

'I seem to be getting quite a lot of hassle returning this lemon of a TV set and—'

'Sir, that warranty isn't valid yet.'

'You what?'

'The No Hassles, No Lemons Guarantee only cuts in after the first year, when the manufacturer's warranty runs out.'

'So you charged my brother sixty dollars for a No Hassles, No Lemons warranty that is absolutely useless. And now, when his set breaks down, you want another fifty dollars on top?'

'I don't think you're seeing things in quite the right way, sir, and—'

'Listen, I came into this place three weeks ago with my brother, and he spent over a thousand bucks on a new fridge and a washing machine. And he bought this set from you eight weeks ago too. I'd say he was a good customer of yours. Wouldn't you say that? He's spent about two thousand dollars in here in the past two months. And now, now, when something goes wrong, you don't honour the warranty he paid extra for, and you want even more money on top.'

'The thing is, sir, the set is a discontinued line and—'

'Not my problem. Your problem. I want this set replaced. At no extra cost. My brother is at home, with a brain tumour. We spent the morning in the hospital where he's having his brain fried with radiation, and on top of that he has to swallow toxic chemicals – so toxic that if he drops one pill on the floor I can't pick it up for him, he has to do it, in case I absorb the chemicals through my skin – and I come in here, with a set he bought in good faith, and you slimy, scum-bagging, grasping, inhuman sons-of-bitches want even more money to replace the crappy TV set you sold him which didn't even last ten weeks. Is that the deal? Is that how you treat people? Is that how you conduct your business? Is that how you treat a dying man? Because, if it is, I'm going home right now to call up every TV station and every damned newspaper I can find to tell them just what dregs of humanity you are.'

I had maybe raised my voice by this point, and the branch manageress, who had been sitting in her office some distance away across the store, left her desk and came over to the counter.

'Chris,' she said. 'Please let the gentleman have the new model. There won't be any extra charge.'

'Thank you,' I said.

'Sorry for any confusion,' she said.

And she went back to her post.

Chris bought the new TV over.

'What about this No Lemons warranty? It has the serial number of the old set on it.'

'I'll issue you a new one.'

'Today's date.'

'Of course.'

I left the shop with the new TV and the new No Hassles, No Lemons Guarantee, and with a new receipt.

A store man held the door for me.

'Thank you,' I said. 'Thanks.'

'No dramas,' he said.

I loaded the TV on the ute and drove home. I was installing it in the sitting room when Louis woke up.

'Hi,' he said.

'How are you feeling?' I asked.

'Wouldn't mind some tea.'

'Make some in a second.'

'Is that a new TV?'

'It is. We can watch a film later.'

'You have any trouble changing it?'

'None at all,' I said.

'Good,' he said.

'I told you it would be fine,' I said. 'You keep saying that we're screwed, Louis, but we aren't, we really aren't. We're not without resources, Louis. We can make a difference. We are not without resources.'

He didn't speak for a second, then he said,

'Did you have to shout at them?'

'Maybe a bit.'

'Yeah,' he said. 'I thought so.'

I left him watching the afternoon news, and went to fill the kettle.

29

WILDLIFE

Going along on Louis' bike, I got punched in the ear. Just like that. Out of nowhere and painful too. 'What the—?'

I stopped and looked around the street. No one. It was deserted. But a bedroom window was open and some curtains were flapping. Some sonofabitch bastard must have thrown something and they were hiding under the sill chortling to themselves now and wondering when it might be safe to look up and take a peek. If I just waited long enough . . .

'Ignorant sons-of—'

Then another punch. It happened again. My ear was ringing and there was blood on my neck.

'What the—?'

I saw the culprit fly away. It was a territorially minded

magpie that had swooped down from a tree and had attacked, to get me out of its neighbourhood, and now it was making doubly sure that I went.

I swiped at it and it cleared off, leaving me free to make a getaway. I stopped at a chemist's and bought some plasters and antiseptic wipes.

After that I started noticing cyclists with cable ties attached to the ribs of their cycle helmets, sticking up like the spines on angry porcupines. I made enquiries and found that this would deter and repel magpie attacks, so I got some and decorated my bike hat with them.

The magpies left me alone then, but the price was that I had to cycle round looking like an alien. But it's a small price to pay for peace of mind. And nothing's really that weird – it's all just ordinary stuff that you haven't quite got used to yet.

People told me that small children had had their eyes pecked out by those aggressive magpies. I didn't know whether to believe them or not, but I kept on my sunglasses.

I got to the hospice and went up to Louis' room and told him that a magpie had attacked me, though he was in a deep coma by now, and probably couldn't hear.

It's an interesting question: what do you talk to the dying about? Do you tell them you love them, do you discuss deep philosophical matters, or do you stick to the everyday, the banal, the benign, the small change and the small coin? Maybe the latter. For surely, even when dying, we still wish to be treated as part of life. We want to know what's going on. Because we're still here, we're not dead yet, and there's time enough for fine speeches and deep thoughts. Maybe we prefer to be included, and not stuck out in some special room, where only hushed-tone matters are discussed.

The hospice café opened at nine, but I would be awake and hungry by five, having spent the night in Louis' room. At seven a café up at Kangaroo Point opened its shutters. This was only half a mile away, so I'd go there for breakfast. The café had tables outside, on the top of the cliff, over-looking the city skyscrapers and the Brisbane river.

The place was always busy, for the runners, the personal trainers, the bikers, the walkers, the t'ai chi types, they would all be there. They exercised together or alone, clad in bright colours and in expanding Lycra, with expensive sports shoes on their feet. The men were mostly bronzed and muscular, the women lean and tanned. They jogged, did press-ups, skipped ropes, jumped hoops.

I don't suppose any of them knew or thought or realised that a short walk away lay those to whom all this health and vigour was irrelevant. Life just seems like a big party sometimes, at which we all gradually get edged to the door, and then we are out in the cold. But the party continues without us, and our absence is barely noticed, and no one wants to look out of the window, at the sight of those departing. For to do so would spoil the fun and destroy the bright, Lycra illusion that this vitality will go on forever and that age can be postponed indefinitely, and if we just keep running and moving, we'll be all right, and some slow-moving old man with a scythe and hourglass will never be able to catch us.

After breakfast, I'd go back and sit with Louis again. The nurses would come and go. Sometimes a visitor might drop by. I'd change the CD. I'd read, do a crossword, get some coffee, sit in the TV room, go back to Louis' bedside. You don't want life to end but you wonder when it will.

The nurse recommended the Old Bridge Hotel to me for lunch, so I walked down there and got a drink and a sandwich. When I bit into the sandwich, I broke a tooth.

When I got back to Louis' room, his friend Michael Meere was there. Michael was Louis' only collar-and-tie friend, with a good job and good money and a company car. They'd met through Bella, many years since, and Michael's wife had had leukaemia, and Louis had helped him out, and now he was returning the favour. He had power of attorney and I liked and trusted him. He was all right.

'I went to the Old Bridge Hotel down the road for lunch,' I said. 'Or I'd have been here when you arrived.' It felt strange only having half a back tooth.

'The Old Bridge Hotel?' Michael said. 'Louis used to work there. As a maintenance man.'

'It was there, was it? Well, well.'

'He said to me, the place is all right for a drink, but whatever you do, don't eat there.'

'Right. I see.'

'How is he?' Michael said. 'Doesn't look like any change here.'

'No,' I said. 'Just the same.'

'I'll call in again,' Michael said. 'I've got to go back to work.'

The days just passed, long and slow. At night, at two or three in the morning, I'd find myself awake, sitting in the now-dark TV room, or wandering the corridors. I'd meet people – nurses, visitors like me, keeping vigil, patients, young and old.

A woman in a T-shirt and a big nappy came into Louis' room. She looked eighty.

'Why have they put the lights off outside?' she said.

'It's night time,' I told her. 'Where's your room?'

She didn't know, so I rang for a nurse.

'Are you a doctor?' the old lady said, as the nurse came.

'No,' I said. 'I'm not.'

I went to the visitors' room and made some tea, then became aware of company, a young woman in a dressing gown, there on the sofa.

'You like some tea?'

'Thank you.'

I made her some and we talked a while. She wasn't even thirty yet and probably wasn't going to see it. She'd been suffering with cancer for over seven years. After a while she went back to her room to try to sleep.

You meet people and afterwards you say to yourself, I don't know what bad luck is, and what do I have to complain about? And yet even then, it's hard to keep smiling, for some reason or another.

The small hours of the morning are like the sea at low ebb, as it moves slowly, restfully, rhythmically – the tide lapping on the beach, the sound of the undertow sucking at the pebbles, the sight of water disappearing into sand.

You see how weird life is, how huge and small, you feel you might even finally get a grasp on it, but then there is the sound of the morning trolley, and the new nurses come in for the change of shift, and the room lights will soon no longer be needed, for you can open the blinds and admit the dawn.

And all those answers you almost had your hand on

have fled again from your grasp. But maybe tonight, maybe tomorrow, maybe one of these days soon, when the world is quiet again, you might understand what it is you need to understand.

But really, you know you never will. And you'll be baffled until the day you die. And even then, you might never find out. You're like an ant crawling over a manuscript. You aren't even aware the words are there, let alone able to read them.

One morning I cycled back from the hospice to Louis' house, to pick up his mail. As I went, I saw that some people had put a stack of papers outside their house for collection by the recycling truck, but the wind had taken them and blown them away.

They were everywhere, hundreds and hundreds of A4 pages, scattered all over the neighbourhood. The couple were going about retrieving them. By the look of it, it would be several hours' work. They were both dressed in office clothes. Maybe they had rung in to say they would be late that day.

The wind was still taking the papers too, and spreading them out over a wider and wider area. But the man and the woman just went on gathering them, patiently, diligently, without apparent anger or irritation, just with acceptance. Not even with resignation – which was too negative a word to apply to how they seemed.

I felt maybe I should stop and help, but I had things to do, so I kept going.

The papers were over the gardens and on the lawns; they were in the hedges and the trees. They paved the sidewalk and lined the gutters. White pages, with the odd line of print upon them. The couple gathered them into bundles and piles, and secured them properly this time, so there would be no more blowing away.

The next day, the papers were all gone, like snow melted from a spring landscape, leaving greenery and not a trace of winter. And you'd never have known they had been there, so clean and tidy were the streets.

30

FLAT WHITE

'I'm just a duffer,' Louis said.

We were heading for the library to renew his membership card. Not that he could read any more, but I couldn't see much point in reminding him of that.

'Who isn't?' I said.

He didn't answer me.

He had trouble getting his library card out of his wallet and I had to do it for him. People on the other sides of counters always know there's something wrong, but they never ask, or want to know necessarily; they may even prefer not to.

'Come here every Sunday afternoon,' Louis said. 'Cycle over and read the boat magazines.'

'Want to look at some now?'

'Maybe later.'

He renewed his membership for another year and we left. He was moving more slowly now, and with an air of distraction, like a man behind glass, peering out.

'I just want to call in here,' he said, as we passed the frontage of a small accountancy office. The frosted glass door was jammed open, to let the air circulate, and inside the room, at the far end of it, a woman at a desk looked up. Perplexed at first, she then stood and came over.

'Louis?'

'This is Pearl,' he said. 'She and her husband bought one of my boats.'

'We lived on it,' she said. 'But David's gone now. How are you, Louis? Are you okay?'

Louis couldn't speak. His eyes filled with tears.

'I'm Louis' brother,' I said. 'He hasn't been well.'

'I'm so sorry,' Pearl said. 'I'm so sorry, Louis. So sorry.'

He went on standing there, misty-eyed, dumb and inarticulate, seeing the past reappear, seeing old times return and as quickly vanish – turned pages, briefly glimpsed, of a snapshot album.

Pearl embraced him, and Louis stood there in her arms, grizzled beard, beanie hat low over his eyes, paint-splattered shorts, scars on his legs and a peculiar disfigurement on the skin of his knees, which I assumed was the result of his roofing days, from kneeling on hot, sun-scorched metal and tiles. Louis wouldn't have bothered with knee protectors. He was tough.

'You take care now, Louis. Keep in touch.'

'How's the boat?' he managed to ask.

'Still good,' she told him. 'Still good. I've got it moored out on the creek. Not supposed to be there. They've moved everyone else on into the marinas. But I sneaked back. I mean, why pay rental when you can moor for free?'

'Good to see you,' Louis said. 'We have to go now.'

'Take care, Louis. And nice to meet you too,' she said. And we went.

Later that day we were back in the hospital. Louis had an appointment with the consultant. The consultant was in his early thirties and he did what he had to as best he could. He was neither patronising nor indifferent; he told you the truth, yet he left a little hope. He did a difficult job well. But then, he did it every day.

'You know the probabilities, Louis?' he asked.

Louis reeled them off. That much he was able to remember easily. The consultant nodded.

'So we just need to wait and see how it will respond to the treatment. In the meantime, if I were in your situation, I'd maybe make contact with the palliative care unit. Just as a safeguard, that's all. Just so that you'll have been in touch if it comes to the point that they're needed in any way.'

After he had gone, we sat in the wheelchairs where we had parked ourselves for the interview.

'I'll shout you a flat white,' Louis said. So we went to the café, and then later we went up to meet the people who ran the palliative care. They were easy-going and pleasant to talk to. It was like you'd gone around to some travel agent's to book a holiday.

'Do you remember Mum's gravy?' Louis asked me afterwards. 'And the soup with all the fat congealing? I used to look across the table at you, thinking, Is this as bad for you as it is for me?'

'You certainly needed to eat that soup quickly,' I said. 'Before it solidified. I suppose if you'd left it long enough, you could have used a knife and fork.'

Louis groaned.

'It's the same for everyone, Louis,' I said.

'No,' he said. 'You think so?'

'In different ways, but in principle. They're all walking down the road, wincing about the past.'

'No,' Louis said. 'They can't be.'

'Let's get some food.'

We tried somewhere new. Louis looked at the menu but didn't say it was pricey, though it was. We sat outside on wicker chairs, lounging back, watching the street life. The waitress brought us food and coffee. The sun was warming. We stayed nearly two hours.

I nearly said, 'This is the life, Louis.' But didn't feel it was the right thing to say.

'This is the life,' he said. 'What do you think?'

'It's certainly nice out here, Louis.'

'Let's get the bill.'

We went back to the house and he slept. The word that kept coming to me was 'uncontainable' – though I was not one hundred per cent sure what it meant, nor, perhaps more importantly, what I meant by it.

But that is what it was and what it is. Life is uncontainable. Our past was uncontainable. The situation we were in was the same. I could not encircle it. It was a thing I could see, but it was like a landscape, I could never put my arms around it, or hold it to me, the way you could hold a baby, a loved one, a child. It was all too immense and too amorphous. All I could do was fetch DVDs from

Blockbusters and make more tea. There was no big red button I could press, to bring salvation running. And even when you have received a death sentence, you still have to live.

Louis collapsed the next day while he was on the phone to the oncology nurse. I was out getting groceries. She sent an ambulance and they took him in. I found him back up on the ward.

'Hi, Louis, how are you?'

'We're screwed,' he said.

And I thought this time he was probably right.

Some things go wrong dramatically and catastrophically, others take the dripping tap and the stalactite and glacier route – slow accretions of imperfection eventually amounting to disaster.

Louis and Bella the sun-kissed blonde washed up in Sydney and things were fine for a while. Louis had a high-paying job with company car and accommodation on the beach front. He worked as a chemical engineer for a water treatment company. Bella worked as a book-keeper. There were barbecues, boats, friends coming round, weekends away. Bella kept horses at the livery stables and rode twice a week. Money, as the saying goes, was no object. And yet it usually is.

But Louis got to not liking the job any more, as was his way.

'It's the arse-licking and the politics,' he told me when he called. 'I hate the damn politics and I'm not licking any arses to get on. And the management are halfwits who don't know what they're doing.'

Only this, I felt, was a refrain heard before.

'I'm thinking of striking out on my own,' he said. 'I don't like working for other people.'

Bella had faith in him back then. All the stars pointed in a propitious direction. She and Louis were still young. He was bright, intelligent, possessed of skills.

'I'm going into stained glass,' Louis said. 'And opening a shop up.'

I still have one of his stained glass pieces hanging on my wall. It was and is beautifully made. But it took Louis a week to make a piece, when he needed to be selling one a day.

The shop did badly and he could not renew the lease.

The company car had gone and the house had gone. They moved up the coast and lived in a small caravan now, on a mobile home park. An awning at the front of the caravan gave them an extra room. In summer the place was stifling. Louis took some stop-gap jobs, labouring and in factories and repairing roofs. Bella still worked as a book-keeper and her regular wage kept things ticking over. She decided to study for accountancy qualifications as her long-term aim. She still had faith in Louis and was supportive of all his schemes. She'd tell her friends what he was doing, and what plans he had.

'Louis is going into boat-building.'

And he built it. But it took six years and much angst and dark nights of souls and black dogs at the heels. He also went into jewellery, and eked out a living that way. But it was only ticking over and they were still living in the tiny caravan. The only way to get a mortgage was to get a regular job. So he went to work in a factory.

They bought the Queenslander. But Bella was losing confidence. Twelve years had gone by and they were in their forties now, and Louis was so long dropped out, he'd have trouble dropping in again. You go and turn your back on the world, it turns its back on you.

Then they split. She lived in the front unit of the house, Louis in the back. She had a vacuum cleaner and a dustpan and brush. Louis did too, but he wasn't one for using them much, as his mind was on other things.

And then there comes a time when you realise it isn't going to be – the things you hoped for and worked towards, they aren't going to come, and life is what it is, and you have to settle for that and resign yourself to it, or sink deeper, and go crazy.

Bella met someone else. So did Louis. Bella moved away and rented her part of the house out. Louis' new relation-ships endured a while and then floundered. The place got dustier, his beard got longer, his eyebrows bushier, the water heater broke down, he didn't get round to fixing it, the years went by, the handle came off his kettle, but he didn't get a new one, rust began to eat the fridge, the washing machine didn't work as it should, drops of paint fell on his clothes, car oil dripped on to his T-shirts, marine anti-fouling spattered his shoes, the beanie hat sank lower on his forehead and began to cover his eyes.

Then one day he called me and said,

'I don't know what's going on here. But I'm having trouble reading.'

Such is life. A lot of people say that, but they don't really mean it, except in a jokey and a wry way. But such it is.

*

233

I met Bella and her new partner, Ted, to discuss the property. I hadn't seen her in thirty years, and didn't recognise her, though she recognised me, not necessarily because I had aged any better, but because I'd always looked this way.

We sat out with our coats on, on a benched table outside the bowls club. We couldn't go inside as some big match was on the TV, and the place was packed with noisy fans.

'I just want to let you know,' I said, 'that Louis is changing the nature of the house ownership so he can leave his share as he pleases in his will. The way things are right now, it would all go to you, Bella, and as you've not been together in over twenty years—'

She looked at me with hostility, like I was a swindler.

'And, of course, the same would apply to you. If you got knocked down or something, your share of the house would go to Louis. You wouldn't be able to leave it to whoever you wanted to.'

'And what if I don't agree to this?'

'It doesn't make any difference. Louis can do it anyway. Same as you can. You don't need the other person's consent. You just make a declaration. Anyway, that's what he's going to do, and he wanted me to tell you. You'll get a letter from the lawyer, but he wanted you to know.'

It was an awkward evening. Bella seemed to be nursing some old bitterness.

'I don't see why this has to be done now,' she said.

'Louis has a brain tumour,' I said.

'I knew a guy, diagnosed with cancer, lived another twenty-five years,' Ted said.

'Not with a brain tumour he didn't, Ted.'

'Knew another guy, diagnosed with leukaemia, lived another fourteen years.'

'Louis doesn't have leukaemia, Ted.'

'Tell me,' Ted said. 'You like books?'

'Some books,' I said.

'Ted likes books,' Bella said. 'He's an avid reader.'

'You know a book called *Mein Kampf* – written by Adolf Hitler?'

'I know of it, of course.'

'You read it?'

'No.'

'Well, I have,' Ted said. He was, incidentally, a builder by trade. 'Well, I have read it, and though it's kind of turgid and heavy going in places, well – he talks quite a lot of sense in there.'

I was going to ask Ted about the six million Jews, but the night had got so chilly I was shivering, and so I said I had to leave and see how Louis was.

Bella didn't visit him in the hospital, nor come to the funeral. Louis left her sixty per cent of the property.

The phone rang one morning. An angry woman shouted down it before I could even say hello.

'You're screwing me,' Bella screamed. 'You're screwing me. Your brother screwed me and now you're screwing me too.'

A copy of the will had arrived for her.

'Bella, what's the problem? Louis has left you sixty per cent of the house.'

'And what about the rest? What about my contribution?'

'Bella, you and Louis split up twenty years ago.'

'What about when I came round to pick up the rates

cheque? Once every couple of months. I'd spend half an hour in there every couple of months, hearing about your brother's problems. Where's my recognition?'

'Bella, I'm sorry, but I don't see why—'

'You screwed up my life! You and your brother, you screwed up my life.'

But none of us really needs any help in that department. We can usually do all that quite easily ourselves with no extraneous assistance whatsoever.

31

SHELL

When you push open a swinging door, then let it go, it doesn't close immediately, but swings back and forth a few times, still permitting access and egress. Then, finally, its energy is used up, and it stays still.

Louis was taken for a CT scan and then an MRI. Despite all that they had thrown at it, all the surgery, chemo and radiation, the tumour was back, regrowing rapidly, even creating its own small blood vessels in the brain, so it could nourish itself. There was NFT – no further treatment.

One day Louis was walking, the next not.

'We're sending you to St Peter's, Louis, as we need the bed here. It's just because we need the bed, that's all.'

They kind of told him, and kind of didn't. They took

him to St Peter's and he got visitors there, and he was giving them bone-crushing handshakes, to show that the strength was still in his arms.

Louis had a deal with his friend Michael Meere that if Louis asked, then Michael would give it to him straight and no bullshit. But he didn't ask. Not directly. He just said,

'I think they'll be letting me out in a couple of days. Feel my grip, Mike. You feel the strength in my hand there?'

'Louis, I think that if you want the doctors to send you home, you've got to show them that you can walk around. I'm not sure you can even walk to the bathroom right now, can you, Louis?'

Louis didn't answer him, just looked away.

And that was how they kept their bargain.

Two days later, Louis was comatose, and the nurses were turning him every three or four hours, to stop bedsores, and I sat with him for a week.

And that's what happens. That's how it is. Just life, taking its course.

They put the wrong date on the death certificate and misspelt his occupation as *chemmical* engineer, and Louis' will went missing. I appointed lawyers and talked to estate agents and I cleared the house, and there was nothing more I could do.

My flight was booked for the Thursday, and on Wednesday night, we all went out to Fried Fish, and I said goodbye to everyone and thanked them for all they had done.

Halley and Don and Mike and Marion came back with me to the house, and we finished off the Little Creatures.

I gave Halley keys so he could come and take the fridge away tomorrow, after I had gone. Then we said our good-byes again, and they left, and I slept for the last time in Louis' house.

In the morning I finished packing and checked I hadn't forgotten anything. The place was an empty shell, just the Salvation Army furniture, waiting to go back to where it had come from.

I checked the cupboards and drawers, in case I had overlooked something. In one of the drawers I found a postcard, of scenery in Scotland. I turned it over. Louis' address had been written in my hand, but the message had been inscribed by a child.

'Dear Uncle Louis,' it read. 'We are on holiday in Scotland. Thank you for my book and my kangaroo which I love very much.'

And under the brief message my daughter had put kisses and signed her name. She is now a grown woman.

Louis had never thrown the card away.

The whole edifice and structure cracked. You think the building you live in is reinforced against earthquakes. You imagine that your carefully constructed tower, built of experience and past adversity, will withstand all hurri-canes, gales and storms. And then a feather flutters down from the sky, and that's all it takes. I sat on the Salvation Army sofa and wept to drown the world.

My mobile rang. It was the taxi driver, saying that he was waiting outside. I put the cases out on the balcony, took one last look, and closed the door. Then carried the bags down to the cab.

The driver was Indian, maybe an illegal, but what difference does it make? We talked about the cricket and the Punjab, where he came from, and the heat and the humidity.

We hit the morning traffic, and I got concerned that I would miss the flight. I asked the driver if he thought we would be all right to get there. He thought we would.

'No worries, sir,' he said. 'No dramas.'

It seems to me that there are – amongst the others – many good and kind people in the world, who do not want you to worry.

But I fear their exhortations might be in vain.

When I got to Heathrow, my wife was waiting. We walked up to the car park where she had left the car. The day was rainy and cold, and I was still wearing clothes suitable for the warm Australian springtime.

'You okay?' she said. 'You chilly?'

'No, I'm fine,' I said. 'I don't feel it.'

For Louis and I were always like that.

We were tough.

32

IN TIME

Louis had some pension insurance that paid out on death and terminal illness. The pension company needed to be reassured that Louis had no living dependants before they would pay the money to his estate. Dependants included any living parents. We had none. But the pension company needed proof that our parents were no longer alive.

I found our mother's death certificate, but not our father's. I did however find his burial certificate. So I sent that in. It proved not to be acceptable.

I called the pension company. They insisted I produce our father's death certificate.

'But you can see from the burial certificate,' I said, 'that he was buried half a century ago.'

'That doesn't prove anything,' the guy taking the call said. 'We need proof that he's actually dead.'

'He's been in a coffin for fifty-plus years.'

'That's not evidence. That's hearsay.'

I got a copy of the death certificate from the government records and posted it on.

I rang up Halley on Skype and told him what had happened.

'It's unbelievable, isn't it, Halley?' I said.

He took so long to answer I thought the line had gone dead.

'She did that trick with a plastic thumb, right?' he said.

'Yes. How's your shed, Halley? How are you doing? How are the bell birds? How's the fridge?'

'I'm going out on the lake with Derek this weekend,' he said. 'Fishing for red claw.'

'What bait are you using?' I asked.

'It's right here in the fruit bowl,' he said. 'You know,' he said, 'I wish Louis was coming with us.'

'Me too,' I said. 'Me too.'

Louis, my brother, always went places first, being older. And then, after a time, I would follow.

I expect he'll still be wearing the beanie hat.

He'll probably say, 'What kept you?'

One of us will know what to do.

The origins of *This is the Life*
Alex Shearer

There is often a fine line between fact and fiction – as fine a line as there may be between life and death – but nobody would pretend that they are the same thing.

Serious illness is a combination of tedium, anxiety and chaos. You sit and you wait; then you panic and get stressed and fraught. And then there is nothing to do again. You are at the mercy of people and events.

To witness someone deal with terminal illness does not require a fraction of the courage that it takes to be the one who is ill. But it is still a fearful and exhausting business. It is a process which demands from you that you come to terms not just with the mortality of others but also your own.

This is the Life is by no means an accurate account by

a reliable narrator. Perhaps no one is more unreliable a narrator than an actual witness to events, who recalls things not as they were, but as they might or should or could have been.

But all the same, the story here is based on experience and on truth – particularly the inescapable one that we are all human and will not live forever.

My own brother fell suddenly and seriously ill, and within a few months he was dead. We were close in some ways, but distant in others. We had known each other a lifetime, yet in some respects we barely knew each other at all.

In extremis all the clichés prove true. Blood is thicker than water. You really do not know what you have until it is gone. Life is too short to quarrel. If you love someone you should tell them so while you still can. And your money is no good in the cemetery.

Books can be rewritten, but lives are only lived once. There can be no revisions: the spelling cannot be corrected; the grammar may not be improved. Yet with all its imperfections, this was a life worth living and worth recording.

Siblings are like no one else. Parents look after us, but we don't grow up with them. Brothers and sisters share our lives in a unique way.

My own brother, like the character in the book, was a talented, intelligent and gifted man – and yet somehow he never did find his niche. I believe that many families have such members. The problem, maybe, is one of a greater idealism and honesty than the rest of us – who are more prepared to make compromises – possess. There are conscientious objectors in peace time as in war, and they too pay a price for not conforming to what the majority do.

'He who neglects what is done for what ought to be done sooner effects his ruin than his preservation.' We had to do Machiavelli at school, and that quote always stuck in my mind. My brother's honesty and idealism did not help him in a less than honest and a materialistic world.

And then there is Robert Service – a mostly forgotten poet, except perhaps for 'The Shooting of Dan McGrew' – who also wrote a poem called 'The Men That Don't Fit In':

> They say: "Could I find my proper groove,
> What a deep mark I would make!"
> So they chop and change, and each fresh move
> Is only a fresh mistake.

My brother showed huge courage and stoicism in his last months. I don't really care for the expression "fighting cancer"; it implies that the person suffering from the disease is in some kind of boxing bout, some kind of fair contest, which – if they lose – implies weakness or deficiency on their part. It isn't like that. People overwhelmingly are not to blame for their illnesses; they are not combatants, they are patients; they are ill. It isn't their fault.

Yet my brother did fight – or at least he resisted; he withheld his consent right to the end. The good night surrounded him, but he did not go gentle into it. He was tough. He was braver than I will ever be.

I returned home after my brother's funeral and felt that somehow it was wrong – it was wrong that he should go, should disappear, should vanish without trace. And so I began to write.

This is not a factual account, but a much fictionalised one. Yet I am proud to have known the person who inspired it, and am glad to have been with him at the end of his life. I miss him. I wish he were here. I always will.